Home

Armand Ferland Sr.

ISBN: 978-1-963153-30-9

Paper Back: 978-1-963153-31-6

Hard Cover: 978-1-963153-32-3

Dedication

To Lori who steered me to finding this book in me.

CONTENTS

About the Author

<u>Armand Ferland Sr.,</u> a native Vermonter now residing in Port Saint Lucie, FL, brings a unique life story to his readers. Growing up as one of nine children on a rural dairy farm instilled in him a foundation of strong work ethics. The challenges of coming from a financially modest background were further compounded by the untimely loss of his mother in 1969, just weeks after his high school graduation.

Armand's journey into adulthood began with marrying Dorothy Lee Hadlock on July 12, 1969, shortly after completing high school. Together, they navigated the complexities of life, raising two sons, Armand Jr. and Christopher, over their fifty-three-year marriage until Dorothy's passing.

Armand's unwavering faith in the Lord Jesus has been a constant throughout his life. In August 1976, he and Dorothy committed to deepening their faith, embarking on a journey that led them to various states. This life of faith, marked by trust in their Savior, eventually brought them back to their native state to care for their ailing parents.

Despite facing health challenges, Armand found success as a construction businessman, working with crews ranging from six to twelve employees. His resilience was tested in 1975 when he contracted Brucellosis (Undulant Fever) from cattle. The road to recovery was arduous, but his faith remained steadfast.

Osteoarthritis, a lasting effect of Undulant Fever, became debilitating in the 2000s, leading to surgeries in 2008 and 2009. During his recovery, Armand rediscovered his passion for writing, producing his longest book, "THE RIDE," in under 30 days. This marked the beginning of his literary journey, where he sought to share life's challenges and highlight remedies received from God.

Armand's writing extends a message of salvation, weaving faith into his characters' lives. While he doesn't work from a structured outline, he allows his faith to flow naturally into his storytelling. Through his books, he encourages readers to reflect on their lives and draw their own conclusions about following the Lord Jesus.

In his parting words to readers, Armand emphasizes the importance of God's love, family bonds, and the pursuit of true wealth without succumbing to greed. His series of five books based on Gideon delves into the Christian life, offering a progression of characters and narratives. Whether exploring crime-stopping heroes or family-friendly fiction, Armand invites readers to enjoy his works and glean insights for living within their pages.

SECRET MISSION: What do you do when you are hearing a voice in your head? Mystery and intrigue become a part of your life whether you asked for it or not. Read how Edna deals with it and prays to remain sane.

SECRET MISSION II: The voice in her head is back and wants Edna to go back into action. Is this the time to disobey or time to continue to obey?

THE SHACK: Homer knew no other life until his uncle told him he was not stupid but unlearned. Homer liked the new life he was being offered but will it turn to greed and destruction.

Page Blank Intentionally

Chapter One

Homer was walking down the road to his Uncle Jake's house. He was going to tend the cattle while his uncle was gone on a trip. Homer knew most of what his chores were, but his uncle had left him a list under the feed bucket near the grain room. The red heifer was to get two cans of grain because she was bigger and older than the two black and white heifers. He was to put out fresh water and half a bale of dry hay for the animals. He knew all this in his mind as he was going along barefoot. He was also going to gather the eggs and give the chickens water and food also.

Homer considered the woods he was walking along and thought that he would like to go fishing later. He watched the blowing of some dead leaves lying in the road as he walked. He kept on walking as a car drove past him and continued down the road. It was the judge's car. He could tell by a political bumper sticker that was bright orange on the rear bumper. He did not like the judge much. He had called Homer stupid one time when he was at a ball game. He had picked up the ball that had been hit by the other team and thrown it to second instead of first. He remembered the people laughing when the judge called him stupid. He did not play ball with them after that incident at that game.

Homer knew he was not very book smart. He had less trouble with his numbers. He could count well and given enough time could add some numbers together. His momma did not care if he did not want to go to school, so he did not go any more. His paw was dead from getting hurt in the mines. He had gotten a bad cut on his leg and by the time the fever set in they could not save him. He and his momma had moved into a shack that was on his Uncle Jake's land when they had to leave the other house because of not having enough money.

Now he was on his way to Uncle Jake's barn and was going to do what he had promised to do. He walked around the last bend in the road, and he could see the barn. The chickens started to cackle when they saw him and were ready to get their grain. Homer told them to wait their turn because the heifers were worth more. He went to the grain room and got the grain to give the heifers. He put their grain in a flat rubber dish and then pushed it under the fence a little bit. The red heifer was in a pen by herself, but all the animals could reach the same big tub of water in their pen. He put some fresh water into the tub and went to get a bale of hay to feed them.

He spoke to the animals as he worked with them and gave them their food. He liked the animals. They did not make fun of him. He finished with the heifers and went to gather the eggs. He gave them their feed and then started to bring the eggs to his Aunt Flora in the house. She was outside hanging some clothes on the line when she noticed Homer coming toward the house. "Good morning, Homer. I did not hear you come. Have you been here a while?"

Homer's Shack

"Yes, Aunt Flora, I have finished with the animals just like Uncle Jake asked me to do," Homer said. "I bring you these eggs, so you could have them."

His aunt replied, "I don't need any more eggs at this time. Do you think your momma would like to have them?"

Homer let a smile come over his face as he answered, "I am sure she would fix them for me if I brought them home."

"Why don't you just bring them home to your momma," his aunt said. "I will get you a bag to carry them home in if you let me finish these few clothes I have to hang yet."

Homer waited by the gate until his aunt brought him a bag. He thanked her and started back down the road to his house. Homer thought his momma would be glad to get some extra food. He was going to set some snares today if he did not go fishing or he might do them both. He startled when a rabbit ran across the road, but he was not quick enough to pick up a stone and try to kill it. He really would have liked to bring a rabbit home to his momma for supper. They did not get to eat meat very often. He had killed a whitetail deer one time, but they could not eat it all before some of the meat went bad. They did not have electricity in the shack, so they had no way to keep meat. They ate as he managed to kill it, but he felt bad that some of the meat had spoiled so he did not kill deer anymore.

Homer and his momma had a garden behind the shack, and they grew some of the food that they had to eat. He and his mother would sometimes go into the woods and get wild mushrooms enough that they could go to the store and trade for things like flour and sugar to fix the other food with. They also dried herbs and roots that were used by others and sold or traded them to folks they knew would take them. They got by and enjoyed each other's company as well as they could. His mother never laughed at him unless he was trying to make her laugh.

Homer was almost twenty years old now. He was bigger than most of the people around and as strong as he was big. He would often get hired to dig holes and such for his neighbors. They would pay him, and he would take the money to his momma because he did not know what anything cost. The only thing that he ever really needed was some new bib overalls occasionally or a nice pair of used pants from the second-hand store in town. He was going to help a neighbor bring in some wood for the fire later this week. He and his mother would get some of the wood in exchange for his work. The neighbor would not let him run the chainsaw, but he would split all the wood as it was cut to length. They had a lean-to off the kitchen door where they kept the firewood to cook with. The neighbor would let Homer put some of the wood on his truck and they would bring it back to the lean to. Momma burned a lot of wood to cook with.

Homer gave the eggs to his mother when he got home, and she cooked a couple of them for him. She put some wild onion and a couple of herbs in the eggs for them to enjoy. They sat together at the table and Homer told his mother all about his morning and having not gotten a chance to kill the rabbit. He told her that he was going to go and set some snares and he would be back in a while. He asked his momma if she would like to go to the pond later today and they could fish for a while. She told him that she would like that, so he said he would be back in just a little while.

Homer knew the woods on his uncle's farm and some beyond. He had walked the woods since he was incredibly young and now the woods were his friend if he had to be alone. There were times when things in his head would bother him. There were times when his mind would create people who were his friends because he did not like to be alone so much of the time. People his mother would read to him about. He loved fairy tales with happy endings, and he would become the hero in his mind. He also loved stories from the bible and how Jesus loved all the people he met. He was sure that he was going to meet Jesus some day and Jesus would love him like he did other folks. Jesus would not care that he was stupid. He was not in the woods to become a hero today. He was trying to get some meat for his mother and him to eat.

Homer had become particularly good at creating little runways for the animals to follow and get caught in his snares. He had learned to use an extraordinarily strong wire that was very thin and slid easily. He would mount his snares so that they would get pulled up into the air and kill the animal quicker. He set three snares today and then went home to get his mother and their fishing poles.

He turned some sod at the edge of the garden and collected a few worms for the pond. Perch was his favorite kind of fish. He liked it as much as trout and better than crappie, so he was going to go to a pond with some perch. The two of them walked silently as they approached the neighbor's pond. It was in the heat of the day and Homer was glad that he had stopped to get some water from the pipe. His neighbor used to keep a horse in the area that they walked in and had a water supply brought over to it, so he did not have to go and water the horse every day.

The sun was beginning to set, and they only had ten perches caught. His mother said they would have to try again on a cloudy day, so the fish could not see them on the bank. Homer reluctantly followed his mother as they walked back to the shack. It was not going to be an excessively big meal tonight. They got back in time that his mother only had to put some more wood in the stove to bring it back to life. Homer cleaned the few fish and gave them to his mother in a bowl. She added a little corn meal and some flour and then put them into the hot grease on the stove. They had a couple of biscuits from this morning, and they shared the bounty that Jesus had blessed them with as they thanked Him for it.

Homer had to go and tend the animals for his uncle before he could go and help the neighbor with his wood. He spoke to the animals as he lovingly cared for them. He even gave the heifers a little extra grain for no reason other than to. He gathered the eggs as he tended the chickens, and his aunt gave them to him again today. He had prepared himself for the blessing from Jesus and had brought the sack with him today. His mother told him that all good things come from Jesus and He was the one that made his aunt generously bless them in His name. On his way home, he went into the woods to check his snares and found a rabbit in one of them. He took the rabbit out and reset the snare again. He went a little way and skinned the rabbit to leave with his mother along with the eggs as he left for the day. It would be nearly dark today when the neighbor would bring him and the wood home.

Homer liked his neighbor Fred Greene who worked for a gas station in town. Fred would have Homer help him several times during the summer. They had already done the first cutting hay for the winter feeding of the cattle. Homer was good at throwing the hay up onto the wagon and then into the barn. He could work all day and not get tired while doing the hay. Mr. Greene would give him a meal when he helped him, and it usually had meat with the meal. There would be other people helping at times who would make fun of Homer. If Mr. Greene heard them, he would make them stop and he even sent one of the men home for continuing after Mr. Greene told him to stop.

Homer was with Mr. Greene to split wood today. They had gotten into the truck when Homer had gotten there and gone to where there were several trees awfully close to the road. Sometimes they had to use a tractor to drag the trees nearer to the road, but they were just going to cut trees near the road today. Mr.

Greene started the chain saw and fell a tree across the road behind the truck. As soon as he had some of the tree bucked into firewood length, Homer would split it into pieces for the stoves. If the wood split very easily, Homer would make the wood fine enough for his mother's stove. The bigger pieces would go for the furnace that was in Mr. Greene's basement. The truck was quickly loaded with the first tree in pieces and Homer started to split the next tree. Mr. Greene would take the first load to the house while Homer continued to split what was cut. Homer would work for hours doing this and not stop except when Mr. Greene asked him to. They had water with them as they worked but they both went with the second load to have some lunch at the house.

Homer liked Mrs. Greene also. She was a rather plump woman who was always smiling and taking care of her children, the house, the animals, or Mr. Greene. She would have Homer come in and wash up for dinner and join them at the table. He loved to play with the little children when he got done with the meal. Mrs. Greene always had food that was quite different from what his mother would fix. They often had loaves of bread that came from a store as well as sliced meat to make sandwiches with. One day she even had a ham from a pig that they had raised. Homer really liked the salty taste of the smoked meat. Today she had sandwiches and some soup from a can. Homer got done eating and got to the floor and the young children climbed all over him until Mr. Greene said it was time to go back to work. Homer thanked Mrs. Greene for the meal and left for the woods again. They did one more load for Mr. Greene and then loaded the load to take for his momma's stove. They drove it to the shack and backed the truck near to the lean to. They tossed it on the ground and Mr. Greene told Homer he would like him to work again next week.

Homer was whistling as he walked to his uncles this morning. He took a special time this morning with the heifers and emptied all the water from the tub, so they would have completely fresh water to enjoy. He gave them their grain and half a bale of hay before he went to tend the chickens. He knew his aunt was gone to pick up his uncle from his trip, so he put the eggs on the steps of the house and left. Homer went home in a different direction this morning. He wanted to go by a pond and swim for a while. It was how he took most of his baths in the summer and he had really sweated a great deal yesterday with the wood. He got to the pond and removed his bib overalls before he went in the pond naked. He was enjoying his swimming so much that he did not hear Rachael Jane come to the pond from a different direction. This was her father's pond, and they knew that Homer would swim in it at times and had never said not to. Rachael said, "Homer, you are naked as a jay bird. I came here to swim, and I did not bring a suit with me either. Why don't you turn around until I get into the water?"

"Why do you want me to turn around until you get into the water?" Homer asked. "We have been here together before, and we had fun splashing each other in the water. Is there something wrong today?"

Rachael insistently said, "I am getting older and maybe I don't want you to see me anymore.

Homer started to be irritated as he said, "I don't know what you mean but I will turn around to make you happy. We have been swimming in this pond for years and I do not know what your problem is. I must go and check my snares in a few minutes anyway and you can be alone."

Rachael took on a teasing tone and asked, "You haven't noticed that I have changed in the last couple of years. Do you know the difference between a man and a woman Homer?"

Homer was about to say mean things but said, "Of course I know that men and women look different, and they wear different clothes. Is that what you mean?"

"Is that all you know about it?" Rachael asked. "There are a lot more differences than that and you might want to ask your momma how we are different.

Homer was getting irritated with Rachael implying that he was stupid the way most people did. He turned around and swam to the place where he had left his bibs and got out of the pond. He was putting them on when he noticed that Rachael was watching him. Homer said, "You seem to like looking at me." He turned and headed for home without another word being said between them.

He went through the woods and checked his snares, but they were empty. He continued to his house and went to his room before he asked his mother what was going on with Rachael.

Chapter Two

Homer was lying on his bed when he heard an automobile stopping by the shack. He looked out to see his Uncle Jake and Aunt Flora stop and getting out of the car. They had a bag with them, and he went out to see what was going on. They had brought them a chicken from town to cook. It was to say thank you to Homer for having cared for the livestock while he was gone for those few days. His momma thanked them, and they were gone in a few minutes. His momma went into the kitchen and Homer started to stack the wood that he and Mr. Greene had tossed on the ground. He was almost done when his momma asked him to go to the garden and get some greens to go with the chicken in the pot. It was the second day with meat in the pot and Homer was thinking that he could do it more often if he had a gun to hunt with. He would ask his momma if he could get a gun somewhere.

Homer went out in the morning and his snares were empty again. He took one and moved it to another part of the woods. He jumped a rabbit as he walked, and he knew he could have shot it if he had a gun. A grey squirrel jumped in the trees over his head, and he could have put that in the pot also. He had walked so far this morning that he had come out on the road on the other side of the woods. He decided that he would go home on the road and have a look around the neighborhood. He had not gone far when he found an unknown woman sitting in her car on the side of the road. He said good morning to her as he walked by and asked her if she was okay. Then he noticed the flat tire on her car as she also told him about it. He asked her if she needed help to change it and she said yes. The woman got out of her car and Homer could see that she was smartly dressed. He went to the trunk of the car and opened it up. Homer had been taught by his uncle how to change a tire one time when they had one on his car. Homer took out her jack and the tire iron and went to the side of the car. He easily loosened up the lug nuts and then lifted the car on the jack. He got the spare tire out before he jacked the car all the way, so he would be ready to apply the new tire. He removed the lug nuts from the flat tire and then swapped out for the new tire. He replaced the lug nuts and then lowered the car from the jack to finish tightening the wheel to the rim. He put all the tools back into the car and put the flat tire in as well. He told the woman that she could leave now, and she put a twenty-dollar bill in his hand as she got into the car. She thanked him, and Homer went to give her back the money. She asked him to please keep it and she left in her car.

Homer could not remember ever having anyone pay him that much for a little work. He thanked Jesus for the money and was thinking that he may be able to add to it to buy a gun. He waved to a couple of the neighbors as he walked along the road. One neighbor offered him a glass of water and he accepted it with gratitude. The neighbor was working in his garden when Homer had waved to him, and Homer decided to help him to hoe the garden before he went along. He had hoed down two rows of beans and the neighbor said that they had done enough work for one day. He handed Homer a dollar to which Homer said, "I did not help for the money." The man insisted that he take it and so Homer headed home again after another glass of water. Before he left, the neighbor asked him if he wanted to come by tomorrow and finish the hoeing for some more money. Homer told him yes, but he was going to come earlier in the day while it was still cool.

Homer was going by the last neighbor before getting to the shack. The neighbor was driving a tractor with a load of hay bales on the back. He waved to Homer to come over to where he was. The neighbor asked him if he would help put the bales into the barn with him and Homer said yes. The barn loft was stifling hot when Homer got there. He would take the bales from the door to the stack and put them into place. They worked for over an hour to put the entire load into the barn. Homer was soaking wet and covered in chaff when he got done and came down out of the barn. The neighbor chuckled kindly at him and offered him a cold drink. The man gave him a five-dollar bill for his help and Homer thanked him and headed home. The man asked Homer if he wanted more work at times and how to reach him to ask him. Homer said he would appreciate any work and the only way was to go by the shack and tell him or his mother when he wanted.

Homer decided that he had to go to one of the ponds in the area and get cleaned up from the hay loft. He did not want to go to

Rachael's Pond in case she was there swimming. He settled for another pond near his Uncle Jake's farm today before he went home.

Homer got home late in the afternoon and his mother asked him where he had been all day. He related his day to her and then he took the money from his pockets. He asked his mother if he could buy a gun, so they could have more meat to eat. She looked at her son and saw how he was trying to help take care of them. She told him that they would put the money aside and see if his uncle would help him buy a gun soon. He then told her about having more work for tomorrow and how the farmer was going to use him also. His mother complimented him on how well he had done today and how he would soon be putting more meat on the table for them. He just smiled as he listened to his mother.

Homer found a rabbit in one of his snares in the morning, so he had to take that home before he could go and finish the garden. He handed it to his mother and told her he was going to work now.

The neighbor did not help with the hoeing today. Homer did the last three rows and was done just before lunch time. They invited him to eat with them before he left, and he was glad to do that. They had a vegetable beef stew with some biscuits on the side with butter. Homer was careful not to eat too much but when they offered him a second bowl, he was glad to accept it. He liked to taste the different foods that his neighbors ate that came from a store in town. The man gave him three dollars today for the work and Homer told him anytime he needed someone he could just stop by the shack and ask for him. The neighbor said he would do that when it was time to do the winter wood. Homer told him how he worked with Fred Greene for some of the wood or he could be paid as well.

Homer followed the road back to the shack and was glad that he did not have to go into the hay loft today. He could see a field of cut hay drying behind the neighbor's house and anticipated getting some more work for the next day. Homer took a minute to thank Jesus for the money and asked Him to help him find a gun to get meat with. In another two days he was going to help Fred Greene again and get another load of wood for the shed. Homer decided that he would like a swim today and took a chance by going to Rachael's Pond. It was deeper than the one he had gone to last night and the shore was much cleaner. He was glad that she was not there when he arrived. He just swam around for nearly an hour before he got out and went home to have some rabbit stew.

Homer and his mother were enjoying their meal when the neighbor with the hay came over and asked Homer to help the next day. The man asked him to come in the morning because he had some other work that he wanted help with. While he was there, he looked around at where they lived and had a thought on how he could help them if they would let him.

Homer checked his snares diligently as he made his way to

the farmer's house. He found the farmer building a fence around one of the fields that he was going to let his cattle graze in now that he had taken a winter cutting off from it. The two of them drove posts and set electric wire around the field until it was time to go and bale the hay. The two men were talking as they worked, and Homer started telling the farmer how he was saving money to buy a gun, so they could have more meat on the table. The farmer just listened and did not say much except when asked why they were doing what they were doing. The farmer had Homer come in and eat with them when it was time. The farmer had a couple of children that appeared to be about ten years old, and Homer started to speak to them after the meal. He ended up going outside to play ball with the boy while the farmer got done his meal. They filled a big plastic cooler with cold water to take with them to the field and get the hay. Homer set a few more posts as the farmer baled the hay. He then went to the barn and got the wagon to pick up the bales onto. He came over and got Homer to help him finish the hay as it took two loads to get it all taken care of and into the loft. Homer was even dirtier than the other night after the second load. The farmer asked him if he could help with the last of the fence in the morning. Homer told him he had to help Fred Greene with wood the next day but could help the day after. That was fine with the farmer, and he also told Homer that he would pay him when they were done on that day.

Homer did not care if Rachael was in the pond today or not,

he had to get some of the chaff off to stop the itching. He went through the woods and there was no one there again today so Homer went into swim. He was tired from the day's work and did not stay as he had the day before. He was just getting dressed when Rachael did come along. They said hello to each other as Homer left for home. He walked through the woods to check his snares and found one had missed its mark. He reset it quickly and went home.

Homer checked his snares on the way to Fred Greene's in the morning. He was angry at not catching any animals for several days and was just going to pull his snares and use some of his money to buy meat. He did not have time to go back to all of them again, so he left them out one more time. Fred was waiting for Homer when he got there. Fred had Homer drive the tractor to the woods this time, so they could get some trees farther off the road. Homer was careful not to hit anything as he drove out to the area in which they were cutting. Fred told him that this should be enough wood for him for this year and if they hurried, they might be able to get two loads for the shed.

The morning went by quickly and they had brought out three loads for Mr. Greene and had one load on for the shed when they went out for dinner. Homer washed up for lunch and was playing with the children when they were called to the table. The two men went and brought the load of wood to the shed and went back for more. Mr. Greene cut two more trees and they made quick work of them. Homer drove the tractor back to the house and put it in its shed. On the way over with the wood, Homer said, "I am trying to make enough money to buy a gun. I want to put more meat on the table for Momma and me."

Mr. Greene asked if he had ever raised chickens or rabbits for meat. Homer told him that he had no wire to build a cage for the animals, so he would have to buy that before he could raise them. Mr. Greene said he had some wire that he could have, and they might be able to lift an old shed by the barn and use it as part of the pens. They decided that they would try to move the shed next week instead of cutting wood. Homer was all excited at the thought of being able to keep some animals for eggs and to eat. It was now time to unload the wood and call it a day.

Homer was telling his momma how Mr. Greene was going to give them a shed and wire to start raising some of their own meat. He asked her what she would like to raise first. She told him that she would like some chickens and maybe a turkey, but it would have to be made tightly to keep varmints out and the chickens in. Homer said he knew he could do that once the shed got there and set next week. He asked his momma if he should raise rabbits also. She only said they would have to see how the money was coming in to buy food with. She said that the shed had to be as far back in the eastern corner as possible to help with the flies and the smell.

Homer was back finishing the fence the next morning. They went all the way around the fields and up to a brook for the cattle to be able to drink in the daytime. They finished the work before they went for lunch. When lunch was over, the boy wanted to play ball again. Homer would pitch the ball and the boy would hit it into the field until it was time to make a connector from the field to the barn with the farmer. They finished the work and went back to the house. The farmer asked Homer if he wanted to be paid today and Homer said it would be nice to get paid, so he could add the money toward buying a gun. The farmer asked Homer if he would like to trade the two days' work for something instead. Homer looked down as he asked what he had to trade. The farmer reached behind the door and brought out a shotgun to show Homer. Homer's eyes got big, and a smile came over him as he looked at the shotgun in the farmer's hands. The farmer told Homer that it was a single shot twenty gauge that he had gotten as a boy. He now had a new one and he could have it and some shells for the two days' work. Homer quickly said he would do the trade. The farmer showed Homer how to load the gun and how to unload it for safety. Homer was as proud of that old gun as his uncle was of his new car and he went home to show his momma.

Chapter Three

Homer had shown his momma the old shotgun when he had gotten home from working with the farmer. He told her that he was going hunting in the morning because he did not have any work for the morning. His momma told him to be incredibly careful to not hurt anyone or anything that he did not intend to kill. He had assured her he would be careful, and she told him to not shoot more than they could eat just because he had a gun now.

Homer went to check his snares first thing in the morning. They were empty again, so he decided to walk along the road toward his uncle's house and try to find a rabbit. He had not gone far when he jumped a rabbit that ran towards the woods. He brought the gun up and fired at the running rabbit, but it did not even slow down. The dirt behind the rabbit went flying up and Homer realized he would have to shoot in front of a running rabbit. He took a careful look with his mind as to how far ahead he would have to shoot and knew he would get the next one. He put another shell into the gun and was about to go into the woods after the rabbit when his uncle came down the road in his car.

His Uncle Jake said, "Good morning, Homer. I see you got a shotgun to hunt with. Did you get anything yet?"

Homer answered, "I just missed a rabbit. I know now that you must shoot in front of a running rabbit to hit it. I traded some work for the gun, so we can have more meat to eat. I want to take care of my momma better if I can. I have been finding more work lately, but I did not have anything for today, so I am out hunting. Are you on the way to town?"

"No." his uncle said. "I came to see who was shooting on the farm. I did not know about your new gun. Can you help me later today with some work? You hunt for a little longer and then you come to the house, and I will have you help me. Okay!"

Homer shook his head yes as he walked into the woods after the rabbit he had missed. He did not see the rabbit, but he found two squirrels in a tree and shot them as they sat beside each other. He dressed them out and brought them to his momma to fix for a meal. He told her that he was going over to help his uncle as he had asked. Homer walked the short distance to his uncle's house and was doing some thinking along the way. His momma and his uncle were brother and sister born to his Grandpa Jed and Grandma Lucille who were as dead as his paw. They had left the farm for their son, but he was supposed to help his sister when he could. That is how they came to live in the shack on the farm. There was a better house on the farm, but his momma did not want to owe anybody in her pride. She knew that no one would ever rent the shack, so they lived there to not owe anybody. His Uncle had tried to get her to move into the other house for years and did not rent it, so she could move in.

Homer was now at the door and his aunt asked him if he wanted some water before going out to meet his uncle at the other house. He had a glass and then went to the other house. This house was old but had electricity and running water in it. You could burn wood but there was a range to cook on and a refrigerator for keeping meat. It also had something that Homer really would like to have and that was a bathroom in the house. He went inside to find his uncle trying to take a broken window sash from its jamb, so he could repair it. They said hello and Homer took a hold of the sash as his uncle pried the jamb as the window came right out. They replaced the broken glass and put the sash back where it belonged after they glazed it. They had to do one more and that one went easier than the first. They put a couple of nails in some loose treads leading to the upstairs and two of the bedrooms. They finished that and then they went back downstairs, and each took a seat in the kitchen.

Uncle Jake said, "Homer, I need your help. I have wanted you and your momma to live here for a long time, but she says she will not take charity. I had a visit from the health department officer the other day. They came to see me because I own the shack that you live in. I do not know if you understand the word condemned or not, but they told me that the shack was now condemned, and no one could live there anymore. It is mostly because there is no bathroom there for you to use and that is against the law. They told me that they would be back in ten days and if it is not empty, they will move your stuff and burn it to the ground. They were profoundly serious about telling me this. I need your help in getting your momma to move in here as soon as possible. It would be so much better for the two of you and you could keep food cold, so it did not spoil. The bathroom works and that would make the health officer happy. You could work for me to help pay rent, so your momma would not feel like it was charity. Can you help me to do this?"

Homer had a puzzled look on his face as he answered, "I understand what you have said for the most part. She can be pure stubborn when she wants to be, but she also has the utmost respect for the law. We will have to make a fuss about the law to get her to move but she will do it. We have no other choice. Are we going home to see her now?"

Uncle Jake replied, "It is as good a time as any. She is going to dig in her heels when we try to drag her out of the shack. I will drive us there, so I can give her a ride to this house for a look. That health officer was serious about burning the shack to the ground if someone was still living there next week. This will be better for her as she gets older like we all do. Your aunt is going to come over if we get her here today and help us talk to her. Let us do it now."

The two of them got into the car and headed for the shack. They went to the next road and turned the car to be going in the right direction when they stopped. His uncle said, "You sit with her in the back seat and make sure she doesn't try to jump out. We both know that she will be mad for a while, but she must do this." They walked to the shack together anticipating a problem. Instead of a problem, she got right in with them to go to the farm. She did not even say a word when they pulled up to the old house. They all walked in together making small talk as they went in and followed by Flora.

Jake was the first to speak, "Sis, I got to talk to you about something very serious."

She interrupted him and said, "I know why you brought me here and it is going to be okay. I ran that town officer off twice before he came to see you. He told me what he had told you he was going to do. He was mad enough at me for holding my ax and waving it at him that I knew he was going to get the upper hand somehow. I don't have any money to pay for this house."

Jake responded with empathy, "We got that all worked out. Homer is going to work for me some. Besides, I promised ma and pa to help take care of you on the farm here. I will just be keeping my promise to them. I am so happy that you are finally going to take our offer and come live here. Flora will help you learn how to use your range for cooking and what to do to freeze meat for the keeping. It will take some learning, but we will all do this together. I will come early in the morning to help move the few things you have, and you can start living here tomorrow."

With that said, they all looked at the house and then they went home to the shack for the night. Much later when Homer was lying in bed, he could hear some soft sobs as he went to sleep praying that Jesus would make his momma feel better.

The early morning sun was streaming into the room where Homer and his momma sat eating breakfast of biscuits and home-made jelly, she had made earlier this summer. She had made a fire to bake the biscuits in but was now letting the stove go out knowing she would not be using it in the cabin again. They were just getting finished as Jake pulled up in his car. He said, "Good morning, Sis. I went and got some boxes from town to put your stuff in to move to the house. I can see that you have been crying but this is a good thing we are doing."

They were all starting to put things in boxes when the farmer Homer helped stopped by. He had two beds that he wanted to give Homer and his momma that they no longer used. The three men went and put them in the two bedrooms of the new house. Homer thanked him for the beds and told him that if he needed help, he could now be reached at the house. The farmer asked him if he still wanted the old shed and the wire to raise food and Homer said yes and he was still planning on coming over to help move them. Homer added how he had shot two squirrels with one shot with his new gun as the farmer left.

The men went back to get a load of boxes from the shack. They put the items into the house and went back with the empty boxes. They filled them again and brought his momma over to the house this time to unload them. Homer tried to encourage her with all the extra room this house had but she just nodded without saying a word. Before they went over for the last load, they stopped at Jakes house to eat some lunch. Flora said, "Come on in and get cleaned up and I will put the food on the table for you. I made some stew with corn bread for you to enjoy. I will come over around three o'clock to show you how to use the range to make your meal for tonight."

His momma sheepishly said, "I think I can remember most of it from when we were in our first house. I will have to remember to not put wood in the side door as it is cooking." They all laughed at her attempt to keep a sense of humor during this hard time for her. "I will need some things from a store to use in this house that I do not have such as bath soap and dish soap."

"I will be glad to take you, or Flora and I will pick it up for you tomorrow," Jake replied. "We normally go to town at the end of the week for what we need ourselves. You are welcome to come with us around nine o'clock tomorrow and we can do it together. When we get done our lunches, we can go and get the last of what you will need today."

The lunches were finished with just some small talk about current events in the neighborhood. They took the boxes back for one more trip from the shack. They had all that was needed and usable and were leaving but Homer's momma said she would walk over directly. Jake motioned for Homer to come along with him and told sis to take her time. The two men put the last of the belongings in the house and were just talking by the porch.

Suddenly, Flora came out of the house yelling "Fire." Homer and Jake looked where Flora was pointing toward the shack, and they could see dark billowing smoke rising above the trees. The other thing they could see was Homer's momma coming down the road. She never looked up as she walked by them and went into the house and closed the door. Jake said, "I think she needed help in leaving."

The shack burned to the point that you could not tell there had been a house there except for where the wood stove stood beside a smoldering wood pile by the time they left for town in the morning. Sis did not turn her head as they drove past Jake's car on the way to the store. She was dressed in a dated light brown dress that hung from her shoulders with only a slight flare at the bottom. She had not cared how her appearance affected people since her husband had died. She had cared once as she proudly stood at the arm of the man she had waited for while he was in the war. He had come back from Europe, and they were married that spring amongst their family and friends in the field by the church. They had bought a house near town where he worked in the mines.

Homer was born healthy after she had lost two children while still early in her pregnancy. He had remained at home for two extra years from the time he should have been going to school. It was during the time shortly after her husband's untimely death and their moving to the shack. The bank had given her time to grieve her husband and then they moved. Homer was bigger than most children his own age to begin with and the smaller children were afraid of the boy who could not seem to learn while he was in school. He had never hurt any of them, but they all knew better than pick a fight with him because of the things they saw him lift. When he was still an adolescent, he helped his Uncle Jake fix a car. It had fallen off the jacks and Homer picked up the rear of the car, so his uncle could put the jacks back under it and finish the work. It did not take many stories like that before people gave Homer a wide berth.

They arrived in town and bought a bunch of items for the house. Flora helped Sis make her choices as they walked the isles. Sis had never seen so many choices of soap for different things. Jake bought a few items for her without telling her including some raisin bread and bath oil beads. He even bought a box of shells for Homer's gun. They finished their shopping and headed back out to the farm. They stopped at Jake's service station and put some gas in the car. He told the mechanic working there that he was going to be bringing his nephew in to help with some things in the garage the next day as he left.

Jake and Flora helped Sis put the groceries into the house and went to their house. As they were getting out of the car, Homer came by with a rabbit he had caught in his snares. Jake asked him to be ready to go with him around seven in the morning to the garage. Homer said he would be ready on time as he continued to walk.

Homer was seeing a side of his momma that he had never

seen. She was prone to being quiet, but this was unusual for her. She kept herself busy in the house or was in the back yard just sitting and staring into the sky. She had not spoken except as a direct answer to a question since they had moved to the farm. She would eat her meal and then go into another room or back outside. Homer tried to get her to speak to him, but it was never more than a couple of words at a time. She would just sit and listen to what he said and do little more than smile if appropriate. At least she had stopped crying at night.

Chapter Four

Homer had not worked at the garage very often in the past. His inability to read made it difficult to give him a job without supervision. His uncle was able to teach him how to mount tires with the use of his machine, but he needed help to balance them. Homer could help with the removal and replacement of parts that did not need much adjustment like exhaust systems and water pumps. He had a natural knack for remembering how something had come apart and how to put everything back. Today his uncle had him doing the alternator on a customer's car with the help of the usual mechanic. He had gotten it out and was putting on the new one when his uncle came to have him speak to a woman in the office. He followed his uncle who said, "Homer this is Miss Brown. She teaches reading to the children in school, and I asked her to stop by today. I have asked her to teach you to read so you can do more work here or somewhere else. She will stop here in the office on her way home, so nobody can see what is going on. She has promised to tell no one about it either. I am going to leave you two alone for a few minutes, so you can meet each other."

Miss Brown walked into the office as she said, "Hello Homer. Your uncle said you were a big man and that is surely true. I would like to know if you know the letters of the alphabet before they make words. Would you please recite the letters as you see them on these cards? They are not in order on purpose."

She and Homer worked in the office for thirty minutes on the letters and Homer was now getting them right. He had become slightly frustrated once, but she got him back on track. She told Homer that she would meet with him when she could, and it would not be every day. She told him to study the cards she was leaving for him, and she would see him on Monday. She left the office and Homer went to finish the work on the alternator. When he was finished, the regular mechanic used a tester to see that it was done correctly. His uncle said he was done in the office, and they could go home for the day. On the way home, his uncle started to speak to him, "I hope you are not too mad about my getting Miss Brown to teach you. I believe that you are much more intelligent than most people think. I could give you full-time work if you could read directions. I spoke to your aunt, and we have decided that I will pay you three dollars per hour in the beginning. The rest that I would normally pay an employee will pay the rent on the house and the utilities. The day that you can read better, I will start to increase your pay. I also need you to be able to count change back to a customer if they buy gas from us. How does that sound to you?"

"You want me to work for you all the time?" Homer asked. "And you want me to learn how to read and write and count money?"

Jake said, "That is exactly what I want. I know that you help some of the neighbors, but you can do that on weekends. I will also get you some coveralls that we can send to get the grease and oils out of them. Do you own some shoes or boots you can work in?"

"I haven't had shoes in years," Homer said. "I am supposed to get a shed and wire from the farmer I help do his haying tomorrow. I want to raise some meat for momma and me to eat. I am thinking chickens and maybe rabbits at first. I do not know where to put a shed for animals now we have moved. I have not seen my momma like this before. She hasn't said a word to me in days and she doesn't do anything around the house."

Jake rubbed his chin as he did when he was thinking and said, "She is just off her routine right now and needs to find something to do. We will start a garden for her as soon as possible. We can put that shed near the woods behind the house for now. I have a good chicken coop and we can share it. We can order some new chicks and separate them with a fence, so we can have some eggs on one side and some meat on the other. Now you have electricity, you can keep meat in the freezer for later or when you need it. We might even be able to raise some pigs together. You ask Sis where she wants us to plow her garden."

Homer left his uncle's car and did not tell his momma about the alphabet cards he had brought home to practice with. He placed them in his room and then went to speak to his momma about her day and to see where she wanted her garden. She told him that it was the wrong time to plant a garden, but Homer said it was going to take time to clean up unturned soil and have it ready. Homer told her that he was going out to pull his snares because he did not have time to check them as he worked for his uncle. He took his gun and went out to the woods to fetch his snares. He gathered up the snares and was going toward the house when he saw a big possum scratching in the dirt to his left. He raised the gun to his shoulder and fired. The possum gave a few kicks in the dirt and then went quiet. He picked up the animal and dressed it out to take it home.

Homer went to his room for a while after he gave his momma the possum he had shot. He took out the cards from Miss Brown and started to practice recognizing the alphabet. He was quickly able to shuffle the cards and still get them right. He found that he had a new desire to become able to read and to help in the garage more. His Uncle Jake had said something that had sparked a flame of hope. He had said that Homer was not stupid but was unlearned. His uncle believed that he could learn and was willing to help him. His thoughts were interrupted as his momma told him that supper was ready and that he should come down. He placed the cards out of sight and went to join his momma. At the table, they discussed putting the shed by the woods and how they could keep some chickens in his uncle's coop. Things really could get better for them.

Homer went to the farmer's house in the morning. They took a saw up to the woods with the tractor and cut three lengths of wood from one tree. They dragged the trees over by the shed and placed them by the two sides. They dug a couple of holes along one side and then used some poles for pry bars. As they pried the shed up, they would place wooden blocks or flat stones to keep it elevated until they did another lift. Once they had it high enough, they rolled the new poles under the side. They put the pole in a couple of feet and then started to raise the other side. They placed the two new poles and then cut a couple of notches in them on the bottom side. They then placed the third log on the first two and chained them together using the notches to place the chains through. Now they had the shed up on two skid poles and they used the tractor to pull all of it from the connecting pole. It worked perfectly, and the shed was dragged to its new home by the woods. They removed the chains and then the skid poles. The job was done. The farmer had put the wire in the shed, so it moved with the shed. Homer thanked the farmer and asked him if he owed him anything. The farmer asked Homer if he could help put up some firewood the following weekend for one day and they would be even. They agreed on a time for next week and the farmer went home.

Homer looked at his new shed proudly for the first time after the farmer left. It was almost too big for a coop, but he knew he could section off one area to keep the feed in. He could put some laying boxes on one side and put some roosting poles in another corner. That is if he did not take his uncle up on his offer and put their chickens in together in the existing coop. Then he could use this for rabbits. He did not have to decide today.

Homer heard his momma calling him and he called back to

her. She asked him to go to the garden that had been by the shack and see if there was anything he could pick to put in a stew with the left-over possum. He took a sack as well as his gun to go and have a look. Homer found a couple of yellow squash that were too old, but they could go in a stew. He also found some green beans that were ripe, and he pulled five of the biggest carrots he could see. He was kneeling by the beans when he saw a rabbit coming toward the garden. He moved slowly until he got his gun. He shot the rabbit and said, "You won't be eating any more of my carrots now you long eared varmint." He dressed the rabbit and carried it along with the sack of vegetables to the house.

Jake and Flora had asked Homer and Sis if they wanted to go to church with them on Sunday. They all gathered in the morning and went to the small church in town for the service. Homer enjoyed hearing about the love Jesus had for his people during the sermons. It was no different today as Homer asked Jesus to help him learn to read so he could get a bible of his own. The service ended with the usual time of having fellowship one with another and Homer got to say hello to Pastor Mike Murray on his way out the door. Jake said he had to go to the store for some sandwich meat and asked Homer to come in the store with him. Homer watched his uncle pick out some turkey breast to be sliced. Jake asked him what kind of cheese he liked, and he had to answer that he had not had cheese before that he could remember. Jake did not say anything as he ordered some cheddar cheese. He also bought a small turkey from the meat case as well as two chickens for baking. He finished the trip with several loaves of bread.

Homer thanked his uncle for letting them go to church with them. Jake reminded Homer to be ready to go at seven in the morning. He then turned to Sis and handed her a chicken he had bought. He told her that they were invited to have supper with them after they got home from work. Flora was going to bake the turkey with stuffing and some sweet potatoes for them to enjoy. Sis finally agreed to come with some prompting from Homer and Jake.

Homer was working on a customer's car when the uniform truck stopped by to get the laundry. His uncle had him come out, so the driver could see what size coveralls he needed. The driver said, "I don't have any that large on the truck today. I can make a special stop on Wednesday to leave them off if that is helpful."

It was settled that he would come on Wednesday and drop off the clothes. Homer went back to work until noon when his uncle called him again. It was lunch time and his uncle had brought him a turkey breast and cheese sandwich with mayonnaise on it also. Homer thanked him as he tasted the sandwich for the first time. The cheese fascinated him. He pulled out a small piece and ate it separately to get the full flavor of it. He liked it and his uncle told him how there were hundreds of flavors of cheese to be tried. His uncle asked him if he expected Miss Brown today. He answered yes and told his uncle how he was practicing at home, but he had not told his momma because she had never encouraged him to learn. Jake did not say a word, but he knew how Sis did not believe her son was able to learn. She had never been willing to see that her wallowing in self-pity had been a major contributor to her son not starting school at the same age as other children. Once the younger children saw how much trouble Homer had in learning, they would tease him mercilessly until he retaliated in anger. He had the extra growth and strength to stay in trouble all the time until he quit going in the second grade. His momma decided it was easier to keep him home and had always taken the stand that he was too stupid to learn. Jake had come to know differently over the years.

Miss Brown came at the appointed time, and they went into the office. She was amazed at how good Homer knew the alphabet in just a couple of days. She had brought some new flash cards with pictures and their words spelled out on them. She explained how she wanted Homer to use them and not try to write them out yet. The first one she showed him was a dog and they said the words and the letters together. She then had him do the same thing with twenty more cards and Homer got all the letters right for all but two of the words. They were out of time, but Homer wanted to continue. Miss Brown told him that he could take the cards home for a couple of days until they met again on Wednesday. Homer thanked her and went to finish putting the tires on the car he had been working on.

Chapter Five

The four of them were just getting done their baked turkey dinner. Flora and Sis picked up the leftovers and were putting them in the refrigerator as the two men finished eating what was on their plates. Homer was finishing off a drumstick when he asked, "What was the red stuff you put on with the turkey dressing? It was incredibly good."

Flora said, "That was cranberry sauce made into a jelly from the whole cranberries. You buy it all made in a can from the store. I sometimes make my own from whole cranberries if I can find them. Do you know how they pick cranberries when they are ripe?"

Homer said, "I don't know where to find them for you, so I don't know how they pick them."

Flora chuckled as she said, "They grow in bogs until they are mostly ripe and then they flood the bogs. The berries come off from the plants and float on the water. Then the farmers skim them off from the top of the water to sell them."

Homer said, "I guess that is why I have never seen them because we don't have any bogs. I like blueberries the best when I can find them."

Flora then asked, "Did you know that you can plant blueberry bushes in your garden and raise your own?"

"I didn't have any idea you could do that," Homer said. Where do you get the seeds?"

Flora gave a little smile as she said, "You don't order seeds. You order some bare root plants from a catalog company, and they ship them to you overnight. You then dig a hole big enough to put the roots into and plant it that way. You will have a good crop by the third year. You will get some in the second year, but they do better the third year. If you plant a dozen plants, you will get several quarts of blueberries and you can freeze them for a later time. My father had some plants in his garden when he had the big house."

Sis interrupted by asking where a pan was stored. Then she stated that it was time to go home so Homer would not be late for work in the morning. She thanked them for the meal and started for the door and indicated that Homer should follow. He did not want to make a fuss, so he went home with his momma. Besides, he wanted to look at the flash cards for a while before going to bed. He did not miss any letters tonight.

Homer was at work changing the brake pads on a customer's car. He asked his uncle at noon as they ate their sandwiches if he knew where he could buy some paper and pencils. He told him how he wanted to start doing the letters of the alphabet on paper. His uncle told him that he would have some for him by the time they went home. Then he got very brave and asked, "Uncle Jake, why is my momma so mad at everything? I think even a witch would be smart enough to leave her alone."

His uncle got a sad look on his face and said, "Homer, she wasn't always this mean spirited. She and your father used to have some good times when they were younger. She became bitter when she lost your father so young in life. She might have met someone after your father died but she did not want to be hurt again. Now the loneliness has made her a bitter woman. She had you to care for when she was mourning your father and she only saw you as a burden. She was not able to retain the love she had for you when you were born. She now thinks that by staying the way she is that it will bring no new hurts instead of trying to find something to feel blessed about. She could have lived in the other house since your father died but she just would not do it. I am not trying to help you because I feel sorry for you; it is because it does not have to remain as bad as it has been. I believe you are quite smart but have never been given a chance to change by learning. I will help you if she lets me and then we may have to have a talk about letting you mature and have a life of your own. All this bitterness will make you sick in many ways. I think you are wise to not let her know that you are learning to read at this time. She would try to stop you like she has done in the past. Did I tell you that I ordered one hundred chicks again and they should be here today or tomorrow? I got some birds to eat and some to lay eggs. We will have to make a partition in the coop to keep them apart as they get older. Have you ever helped with young chicks before?"

"I haven't seen chicks before," Homer answered. "I have

been told that they are cute but stupid. Thanks for talking to me about momma. I don't know what to do to help her."

Jake patiently said, "We cannot change her. She will have to come to the point where she wants to change, or she will die a bitter young woman. Chicks are cute, but they are stupid enough to stand on each other until one of them dies if they are scared. You just must move slowly as you take care of them in the coop. The layers are going to be Rhode Island Reds and are red in color as their name implies. The meat birds are going to be White Leghorns and they are white. It will be easy to keep them apart as they grow older. Right now, we must get those tires back on that car, so the customer can drive it home."

Homer was just getting the last tire on when his uncle came back with several pencils and some lined paper for him. He kept them in a bag and put them in the back room. He took two sheets of paper and a pencil and placed them in a pocket to take home.

Homer and his uncle stopped at the store on the way home. His uncle gave him five dollars and told him he could bring some food home to his momma or just for himself. Homer went to the deli and bought some sliced ham and cheddar cheese. He also got a loaf of wheat bread and a quart of milk. The last thing he bought was some biscuit mix for his mother. When he got home, he brought the items in to his momma and showed her what he had bought. He showed her the directions on the box of biscuit mix, and she told him that she could read them. Homer only stated that he was trying to make it easier on her with him being gone so much of the time. He turned his back on her and went to his room.

Homer had a small table that he had brought into his room to place a lamp on, so it would be closer to his bed. He took the pencil and paper out of his pocket and got the flash cards out of hiding as well. He took the pencil as he remembered between his thumb and index finger and started to make the design of the letters in the words on his paper. It did not seem as hard as he remembered it to be as a child. The many years of hard work had taught him how to use his hands with greater ease. He wrote out several of the words before his momma called him down to eat. He put everything out of sight and went downstairs.

When he got to the table, he got the closest thing to an apology that he had ever gotten from his momma. She told him how she knew he was trying to look after her and she appreciated it. She had gone to the garden and gotten some vegetables to put in a stew with the chicken they had brought home on Sunday. She told him that she had been studying the land and the amount of sun that was in behind the house and she told him she had put some stakes in the ground where she thought that it would be best for a garden. Homer told her that they would get it tilled as soon as possible. It was the first time that she had spoken in a decent manner since they had moved into the house.

Homer was having some trouble figuring out how to preassemble a part he had to replace on a car. The other mechanic was busy on another car, but Homer asked him if he knew a trick to putting it together. Without looking up, he asked Homer if he had looked in the directions. Homer started to get angry but decided he would look at the directions that had come in the box. There was a picture diagram of how it was supposed to be held and the way to press the parts together. Homer noticed that the motions in dotted lines were numbered and had a list below the picture with words about how to place them. He took the parts and made them match the diagram on the paper. He proceeded to take the parts with the first number and move it as the dotted line indicated for him to do. They went together so he took the next piece and again followed the lines until they were in alignment. He quickly had it ready to install into the car and proceeded to do just that. He had never done anything in this manner, and he was going to tell his uncle when he got back. He was not sure where his uncle had gone.

The uniform delivery person came around noon and had five pairs of coveralls for Homer to use. The driver explained how he would take two sets to wash each week, so he would be returning two sets and picking up two sets while Homer was wearing the fifth pair. Homer went into the bathroom and came out wearing the first pair for the afternoon's work.

Miss Brown came at her usual time. Homer had her watch as he took a paper and pencil and made the letters to the words on the flash card. She did tell him how to perfect the movement of his hand to make the letters clearer. She also told him that she was amazed at how well he was doing. Homer did admit that they were trying to teach him some of this when he quit going to school when he was younger. When they were done, Miss Brown said she was going to bring some beginners reading books for them to look at. They were just getting done when his uncle came by to take him home.

They were going home when his uncle asked if he had wondered where he had been all day. Homer replied that he had noticed that he was gone. His uncle told him that the chicks had come early in the morning, and he had to take them home and let them out of the box right away. He had rounded up some watering pans and bought some grain for the new chicks and brought them to the coop. He had closed off some of the windows, so it would stay warmer in there until they got older. When the two men got to the farm, they went out to see how things were going. His uncle reminded him to go slow around the chicks as he wanted to pick one up and see how they felt. Homer said they were as soft as rabbit fur with long legs. His uncle smiled at the comment. The chicks had located the feed and the water, so they left them for the night.

Homer was helping the farmer make his wood that Saturday to help pay for the shed and the wire. He was telling the farmer how they had bought one hundred chicks already and had them in his uncle's coop for now. He also took a chance and told the farmer that he was taking reading and writing lessons with the help of his uncle. The farmer asked him if he had any books that were made for learning to read yet. Homer told him no and that he was using the teacher's books when she brought them. He said his uncle called him unlearned and not stupid like most people. The farmer said he had to agree with his uncle and wished him well. They stopped for lunch on the second load of wood to the house. The farmer's son was being asked to pile the wood in the shed once they placed it on the ground. Homer started to help him, and the farmer would not let him. He said the boy was old enough to do some safe work around the farm and this was part of his chores.

Homer enjoyed some home-made beans and salt pork for lunch. They also had some bread right out of the oven with butter. He was happy to see the wife bring out a fresh blueberry pie for dessert. Homer said thank you for the meal and went outside to wait for the farmer to get done. Homer was surprised when the farmer brought him out some early childhood reading books and told him he could use them for a while if he wanted. He told the farmer that he would take good care of them. They managed to get three more loads of wood down before it was too late. The farmer thanked Homer and told him he could keep the books if he needed them. He then gave him a ride home so Homer could show him his chicks. The last thing the farmer asked him was if he wanted to work the next Saturday making wood for pay and Homer said he would see him then.

Homer continued to hide the books and other reading material from his mother. He would spend some time every night studying his letters and trying to recognize words he did not know yet. Miss Brown came on a regular basis and by the next Friday he was able to read one entire book with no help.

Homer found some old two-by-fours and was making his shed tight enough to keep chickens in. He brought home a couple of wooden boxes he had found that parts had come in at the garage and turned them into nesting crates. He went into the woods and got some young saplings to use for roosting bars. He also cut some posts to make a small enclosure that they could go outside in with some wire over the top to keep hawks away from his chickens. He fashioned a box that he could put laying mash in from the top and the chickens would eat out of the bottom. He took some of his money and bought a watering trough for the coop. In a couple of weeks, they could separate the two types of chicks. The white leghorns were already getting larger than the laying hens. His uncle showed him how he could tell that they had gotten a couple of rooster chicks with the layers, and they could leave them in with the meat birds for a while.

Saturday morning Homer was back at the farmers making wood. They had been working most of the day and the farmer felt he had enough wood for the winter. Homer was about to go home when he asked the farmer if he would like to trade with him this time. The farmer asked what he needed, and Homer told him about the garden spot that had never been tilled. The farmer said he would be glad to prepare the soil with his tractor and big rototiller. He asked if they knew where they wanted it and if they were ready and Homer said yes to both. They went over and hooked the two machines together, so they could go over and till the garden. His momma looked out of the house when they got there and came over to show them exactly where she was talking about for the best sun. The farmer tilled over the soil in two directions to cut up the sod as best he could, and he told Homer that if he had some old plastic, he could cover the area and it would finish the job of killing the grass. Homer thanked him for the trade and the farmer went home. Homer noticed a bunch of fish worms coming out of the sod that they had just turned over, so he got a can to catch them into. He told his momma that they could go fishing tomorrow if she wanted to come with him. She said that it might be a good day to go fishing because she expected it to be overcast.

Homer and his momma were fishing in a nearby pond the next afternoon. It was a day made perfectly for fishing. It was overcast and sprinkled a couple of times while they were there. The late season grasses were swaying in the gentle breeze as they sat there quietly catching bluegills for their supper. They caught enough to have a good fish fry and then slowly walked home. His momma caught him by surprise as she asked him how he was doing with his reading.

Homer nervously replied, "I thought that I had kept all that stuff hidden when I wasn't using it. I am doing very well and can read some books by myself."

His momma confessed, "I didn't find it, but you have never talked to yourself in your life, so I listened to what you were saying in your room. I could tell you started with the alphabet and are now in beginner books for reading. You seem to be doing well with it. Pretty soon you won't need me to take care of you anymore."

Homer responded in an angry voice, "I am not doing this, so we will not be together. I am doing this, so it can be better for both of us. I do not know why you have been angry for all these years, but I wanted to see you happy again. I know that I am not as stupid as you want to believe, and I am going to continue learning to read. I liked it the other day when I could look at the directions about how to put something together and read some of it. I like the new house and being able to use the bathroom. I like it when I can go to work every day and make some money to feed the chicks with. We may be able to sell eggs and help to pay for the grain to feed the meat birds. I like the fact that I have tasted cheese, ham, cranberry sauce, and want to try more things because I can buy them for us. What is so wrong with that?"

His momma defensively said, "You think I am an angry woman, but do you know how much I have been hurt in my life?"

Homer was starting to let the anger rise in him as he said, "It has been over fifteen years since daddy died. You did not have to be alone all these years. You just had to want to change but you seem happy being angry and feeling sorry for yourself. Anyone that knows you knows how you have lived your life and how different it could have been. I want things to change momma. I want to be different, and I mean to have things get better for us whether you change or not."

By now his momma was crying softly as she walked along. She did not say anything for a long time. Finally, she said, "Do you think I can change my life at my age? I don't know why you just don't leave home and allow me to be who I am?"

Homer again replied in a raised voice, "Aren't you tired of feeling sorry for yourself? I probably could leave home if you wanted me to, but you are my momma, and I am changing. I am going to make some better things happen and I want you to share them with me. Uncle Jake is trying to do what he can, but you do not make it easy for us. You now have a refrigerator and range and can bake all that you want to, but you do not. You can change anytime that you decide that you want to. You might as well try it because you're not happy the way things are right now."

They were home by now and Homer started to fix the fish for frying. His momma got out some flour and corn meal to batter them with as she heated up some grease on the range. They were eating the tasty fish in no time at all and enjoying it. When they were finished, his momma asked him to bring down one of his books and read it to her. Homer did as she asked, and they read together for over an hour as his momma helped him put the words in order and helped him pronounce them. Homer noticed the time after a while and decided he had to get some sleep before having to work tomorrow. As he left the room, Homer said thanks to his momma.

Homer told his uncle part of what had happened the day before on the way to the service station. He also told him how his momma knew he was trying to learn to read and how they had read for an hour. His Uncle asked, "You really told her all those things on the way home from fishing? Then she read with you after supper. I may not know my Sis the next time I see her if she happens to have a smile on her face."

Homer smiled at his uncle at the thought. They were now at the station and they both had to go to work. The day went well, and Miss Brown came in the afternoon. Homer had to tell her how his momma had found out that he was learning to read and how she had read with him the night before. Miss Brown said that if she really were ready to help, she could read him some words, so he could spell them without looking at them first. They tried it for a while so Homer would understand what she wanted him to do. The part that his uncle liked about the session was that Homer could laugh at some of his mistakes instead of getting angry as he had done in the past.

Homer always liked the ride home on Mondays because his uncle stopped at the grocery store on the way home. This week he took some of his money and bought a good-sized smoked ham. He bought some eggs and flour and a few more things such as shortening for his momma to bake with. He also bought a sack of freshly picked potatoes and a gallon of milk. The last thing he bought was some sliced cheddar cheese and some bologna that his uncle told him he would like for sandwiches. He had high hopes that his momma would think more of the groceries that he bought this week. When they got home, he carried them into the house and his momma put the stuff away and he put the sack of potatoes in a corner of the kitchen. She told him thank you and said she would ask Flora how to prepare the ham and maybe have them come over for dinner that night.

They had the last of the fried fish with some fresh biscuits that his momma had baked that day. When he was still hungry after the fish, Homer sliced off a piece of bologna and put it in a biscuit to eat like a sandwich. As an afterthought, he added some cheese and found it to be excellent. He had not had milk to drink at home on a regular basis and it tasted good with the rest of the meal. When they were done, and the table cleared, Homer told his momma what Miss Brown had instructed him to do with her help. Homer got a pencil, paper, and a book ready at the table near his momma. They worked together for about an hour before Homer went to bed.

Chapter Six

Uncle Jake and Homer were in the coop separating the chicks. Jake asked if he knew that if they kept the Leghorn hens separate, they would lay eggs as well as the Rhode Island Reds. Homer asked why they had gotten two breeds then. The two breeds will be about four pounds different in size and the reds would not get as much mash as they would need. The whites will always use more feed and the results are not that much better unless you want the meat, and we do. When we start to eat them, we can kill the roosters first and see if we end up with some large white eggs someday. They would put around six chicks in the box they were using and take them over to Homer's new coop. It was an interesting project as they got more and more of the reds out but still had to catch the balance. They ended up bringing in an old door and using it as a gate in the corner, so they could corral them all at once. Sis came over to have a laugh at them chasing those chicks. Jake was amazed at seeing her outside of the house and with a smile on her face.

On Sunday, they went to church together to hear the sermon by Pastor Murray. Sis had pulled her hair back, so you could see her face and it was not a sour face as usual. She spoke to several of their neighbors while she was there and was friendly. Then they went to the store to get some groceries. Sis and Homer had spoken before, and they were going to use some of the money and buy some things to bake with and some meats and cheeses. They found some fresh sweet potatoes and some squash in the produce aisle. They got several things to bake with including some canned preserves to make a pie with. They spent more than they had ever spent in a store that day.

When they got home, Homer said he felt like going for a walk with his shotgun and seeing if he could still find some meat. His uncle told him that he had seen some turkeys in the field behind his house the other day and he might want to try and find them. His uncle told him to remember that they could see a lot better than he could and the best thing was to get in front of a turkey in the direction in which he is walking and waiting for him to come by in range. Homer thanked him and went off toward the field. It was a warm autumn day, and the leaves were starting to change colors and woods were coming alive before putting on their drab winter grays. Homer followed the tree line going away from the house. He then entered the woods on an old logging road that paralleled the edge of the field. He stopped to listen occasionally, and he knew that he could hear a turkey hen clucking near him. He went a few yards farther and stood beside a forked tree for a while to see what would happen to come along. He knew to just use his eyes and his ears and not move his entire body as he looked. He could hear the hen scratching at the forest floor near him and coming closer. He moved just enough to have his gun pointed in the right direction to the noise he was hearing. Suddenly, a large tom came out from behind a bush about ten yards away. Homer leveled the gun at the tom's head and fired. He thought he was going to have to shoot it again as it flopped around but he saw that he had shot the head off and there was no need to shoot again. It finally settled down and Homer could see his prize laying there before him. He had never seen a turkey this close before and he played with the wide fanning tail of the bird he was holding. He dressed the bird right there in the woods but left the feet on it to help carry it home. He hoped that his momma would be pleased with him.

He knocked on his uncle's door and showed him the turkey on the way by. They spoke for a few minutes about how he had shot it and where before he took it to his momma. Her eyes got big and wide as she saw the turkey for the first time. She said that she did not think that he could really shoot a turkey on his first try and now she had to make room for it in the refrigerator until they wanted to bake it.

Homer got cleaned up and went to check on the chicks in the new coop. They were doing fine and were starting to lose their downy feel when he picked one up. He put it back down content that they were doing fine in their new coop. He gave them some fresh water because he wanted to and not because they needed it. He then latched the door behind him and went into the house for the evening.

The evening time of studying words and how to spell them was beginning to be different because his momma would give him words that he had not seen yet. The first word was chicks and Homer did not have a good idea of how it went. His momma explained the sounds of the "ch" makes when spoken and then she added the word church with it on both ends. Homer told her he understood, and they tried to come up with some other words with the same letters and sounds. It was not long before she had him write an entire sentence and how to punctuate them. There were basic times of exasperation on Homer's part, but he knew it would have significant benefits to see it through.

The other part of his life that he was improving was the depth of knowledge he was gaining about cars. He was getting surer of himself and rarely had to get help with the basic stuff. He had learned how to balance tires on their rims and could do almost any brake systems the cars had. When he had to, he could help pump the gas for customers and he was always careful about making the right change. People who had known Homer for years were amazed at how things were going for him. People would speak to him in a normal way and many who had called him stupid were more careful with their own tongues while they were around him. One of these people was Flora's dad, the judge, who had called Homer stupid in court one day. They had even spoken at the farm one day when they had come to visit Flora and Jake, and both knew it was different between them.

The weather was starting to change with the onset of autumn and then winter. The trees had become barren, and the winds had a bite to them if you were outside. Homer would put all the chickens into the coop and close the door, so they would stay warmer during the cool evening. The ducks and geese could be seen flying overhead and the last of the farmer's crops were in the barn for the next few months' use. Homer had gone with his uncle to the next town one day and had gone to a second-hand store to get some warmer clothes to wear. He was so proud of himself when he could give his momma a stylish brown coat with brown round buttons on it that she could wear to church.

They woke the morning of the first snow of the year and his uncle was in a hurry to get to the shop. He told Homer that they would probably spend the entire day selling and changing tires for people who had procrastinated until the snow started to get tires. They arrived at the shop and his uncle was right. He worked on tires all day long and even had to stay a little longer than usual to finish two for a customer. Homer was glad that it was not a day when Miss Brown had been scheduled. He had taken just a few minutes to eat his sandwiches and had gone right back to work. He had never seen anything like it. He asked his uncle at the end of the day about why people were so foolish as to put off changing tires before it snowed. His uncle told him that it happened every year and was probably not going to change anytime soon. His uncle had stayed there all day just to give prices and take people's money. He had even pumped gas for customers, so the guys did not have to stop what they were doing at the time.

The next day was not as hurried, but tires remained the main subject of need for their customers. Miss Brown had to wait a few minutes for Homer to finish the customer he was with when she came. Homer was now at the point where they could pick up almost anything and start to read it with some occasional help. She had brought him a dictionary to use to find out what some of the words meant as he read them as well as teaching him the tenses of the sentences. One day his uncle brought him a book on the laws of the road, so he could start practicing for his driver's license. Homer said that he had never dreamed of learning to drive before but he made up his mind that he was going to do it.

Homer had changed the feed for his chicks from growing mash to laying mash as they neared the time to start laying eggs. The leghorn hens were at least a pound heavier than the reds and the roosters were still growing. It was almost time to start eating some of the bigger roosters in the coop. The coop was too small for a flock of big chickens and the roosters were starting to feel the need to create dominance as far as the hens being in with them. The crowded space was making the sparring become quite frequent. They took the six hens and put them in Homer's coop to see how the two breeds were going to act together as far as feed and such. It took a couple of days for the spats to stop but it was soon well in the chicken coops.

Homer was studying the handling of a car as he and his uncle drove back and forth to work. He was combining that with the reading of the driver's manual to prepare himself to learn to drive. Miss Brown was only coming twice a week now and he was doing more with his mother and his uncle while they looked at instructions for certain parts. The acronyms used to adjust a car in the instructions were confusing for a while until his uncle showed him what they were doing. He learned things could be found somewhere on a page to tell him what they were, and it became easier for him to understand. His uncle had been good to his word and was giving Homer more money by the hour. The other thing he was doing was to give Homer his pay and let him and Sis take care of what they wanted and needed instead of just paying the way and his not learning any of the details.

Homer and his momma had started to experiment with foods they could buy at the store, and she also increased her baking. Homer was glad to have more meat to eat but he also enjoyed the pies and cakes that his momma made for him. When the wild berries had become ready in their area, Sis had gone out in the day and picked some for them to enjoy. Homer thought his momma was telling him a story one day when she told him that she had stopped and spoken to the farmer's wife as she had been walking the road to pick berries. Homer said, "Momma, I don't remember you speaking to anyone outside of a church building except for Uncle Jake and Aunt Flora or if someone stopped at the shack looking for me. Did you like her?"

His momma said, "Of course I liked her. She and her

husband are hardworking people and are raising two children. They all like you and the work that you do for them. She said that you have fun playing with the young boy every time that you are there for a meal. I am glad in one way that I only had you to care for when your poppa died but I am sure that you have had a lonely life because of me. We have never spoken about birds and the bees, and you are growing up. She gave me a few fresh carrots and I picked a few more as I passed the garden at the shack. I am going to have to go over and pick the turnips this week and a few of the herbs that I need to dry for winter."

Homer looked at his momma with a look of surprise on his face. He had been praying that Jesus would find a way to make his momma less angry and sad and He was doing it. Homer said, "We have both lived our lives alone and I don't find much pleasure in it. I can tolerate it as I have for years but I do not like it. I do know that Rachael no longer wanted me to see her naked this summer, but she always looked at me. I never tried to hurt her or anything, but I stopped going by her pond if I thought she might be there."

His momma swallowed hard a couple of times and then tried to get him to understand the physical differences between a male and a female. She then made a couple of awkward statements about how human couples acted to have children. Homer just let her speak and did not ask anything while she was speaking. He did ask a couple of questions as she finished but did not go into the matter very deeply. The conversation was quickly over, and they both went to do other things.

Chapter Seven

Homer was gathering the eggs in the morning from the chickens that had started to lay as time progressed. One day a week, they would bring some fresh eggs to the store and trade them for other items that they needed or wanted. His momma was putting eggs with all kinds of meat for them to eat and usually some dried herbs and such for added flavor. She would also bring some over to the farmer's wife on occasion when she went over to be neighborly.

Homer had gotten a car that a customer had for sale one day. It was a nice sedan at one time, but he had hit a tree on the side of the road on some ice and did not want to fix it for himself. Homer had gotten some used parts to repair the front with and was starting to drive it around to get the feel of it. It also needed brakes, so Homer installed them on his own time. He had passed the written part of the license exam for driving and was looking forward to having a car to take the test with for the driving part. He had the test scheduled for the following week in the next town. He was far more confident in himself than he had ever been in his life. He could read most of the books that Miss Brown had brought him and usually could read the directions for putting in an unusual car part. Homer had decided to have the lessons stop with Miss Brown and she also felt that it was a good time to stop coming. She told Homer that he was reading at an eighth-grade level in just a few months of determined effort, and he could continue at his own pace. She had given him a book by Mark Twain as a gift and signed her name in it with some encouraging words.

Homer was riding home with his uncle on Friday night after work and there was a strange car over by the house with some children outside playing. The children looked at Homer as he walked over but they did not say a word as he went into the house. In the house, there was a man and a woman a little older than he and an older gentleman speaking to his momma. They all turned to look at him as he entered, and his momma asked him to come over and meet them. She took him completely by surprise as she said, "I would like you to meet some people that used to be a part of my life a long time ago. I lost tract of them after your pa died but I decided that I would try to send them a letter a while back. They did not answer the letter but decided that they would come over and see us. I have asked their forgiveness for shutting them out of our lives and they were glad to do that. I would like you to meet your uncle Stanley who was brother to your pa. This is his son, James and his wife Elizabeth and they would be your cousins. Their children are outside playing now."

Homer had shaken the hand of each one of them as they were introduced and did not know what to say. His momma started again, "I have told them that you may not remember them, and I have not mentioned any of them for several years. They still live in the next county where I met your pa. You had another cousin that was killed in the war while in the army, but I did not know about that until today. They have waited for you to come home so they could meet you."

Homer still stood in silence as the reality of what his momma had said started to sink into his mind. His uncle was talking with his momma about times that he was not around for and had never heard about. The new cousins questioned him about his work and the farm, but Homer did not tell them much now. He did not know how to answer them because he did not feel any attachment to these people. The years of living alone with his angry momma and hurtful folks in school and town had given Homer the defense of being silent most of the time. He did not have a history to rely on as far as dealing with these new people.

The conversations seemed to dry up and they all piled into the car with promises of returning soon on their lips. Homer and his momma waved to them as they drove down the road. Homer just turned around and went up to his room for a while to think about this. He heard his momma say that his meal would be ready in a few minutes, and he could come down to eat. His nerves would not let him eat much while they were at the table. He finally said, "I don't know what kind of life I would have had if pa had lived but I really don't know what to think about some things. You did not think that I should have known that there were other relatives out there for all those years. Are there more things that I must wait to find out about when you are finally ready to tell me about them?

Did you make me live alone on purpose, so I could feel as lonely as you did?"

Those words made his momma slap down her fork and go running into her room sobbing. Homer got up from the table himself and went back to his room. He knew that he had hurt his momma but this time he was the one that was angry. They did not speak to each other the rest of the night, but he could hear his mother sobbing softly as she worked downstairs.

Homer got up the next morning and left the house in silence. He walked down the road for a way and suddenly found that he was talking out loud to himself as he went. He was still angry with his momma and was arguing with her as he went, and she was not even there. He turned around and started back toward the house. His uncle was out by the coops as he went by, and he started to speak to him. He said, "Uncle Jake do we have other relatives that I do not know about?"

His uncle said, "My only other relatives are on my wife's side of things. The judge is her father, and she does have one older brother who is in a town that is fifty miles away and does not come to visit very often. He is married with one son, but we do not know where he is now. He is in the military and is stationed somewhere in Europe. Why do you ask?"

Homer raised his voice a little as he spoke and said, "Those people who were at the house last night were my Uncle Stanley and his family whom I have never even heard of in my life. Momma just introduces them like I should have known them all my life and be happy to see them. I have been alone with my momma most of my life and I did not know those people existed as part of our family. It made me angry to think about that."

His uncle was slow in beginning to answer, "We have spoken about how angry your momma has been since your pa died. She became what the world would have called depressed and could not help herself out of that place. We have both seen a great deal of change in your momma since she had to leave the shack and move in here. You were already hungry for life to be more than it was like at the shack, and you were ready to learn, taste, see, and feel things that were new. Sis came along kicking and screaming in silence doing things like burning the shack, so she could not go back there. It took her almost a month to get off the back porch and stop staring into the woods. The one good thing that has happened is that while she was staring into the woods, she finally saw the trees. What I mean is she started to see people again. She started to see how I have been trying to help her since our parents died but she could not see it. She has seen you change the most in her own mind. You were a baby that she had to care for when your pa died, and she did take care of you, but she did not care about you for a long time. She is finally seeing you as a young man and as capable a provider as your pa was. Part of what is happening in her mind is the fact that she no longer needs to care for you, and you are caring for her. She can accept that more easily than when I was trying to get her to move into the house because you do not represent an act of pity but of love. I was trying to do it in love, but she could not see it that way. Didn't you tell me that Sis is going over to the farm and seeing the woman and her children at times while we are at work? That is a major change in her approach to life and she is still trying to make some of it fit in her mind. The fact that she wrote to your Uncle Stanley is enormous in her mind in two ways. The obvious thing is just doing it but the second and equally important thing is she is trying to make amends for the lost years. You will have to help her make amends to other people and yourself by being able to forgive some of the things she has done and continues to do. Do you think you can do that?"

Homer just stood there listening to his uncle speaking. He had great respect for his uncle and was taking some time to respond. He finally said, "She is trying to apologize to the world that she has acted the way she has is what you seem to be saying. She knew better but could not change how she felt for those years on her own. I know that I have prayed to Jesus to help her be less angry and now I don't like the answers to my prayers."

His uncle smiled and said, "That is one way to look at it. Jesus tells us that we must go to our brothers and sisters and ask for forgiveness for the things that we have done wrong to them. I find it amazing that Jesus is answering your prayers in such a powerful way. You are getting a new momma and I am getting my old sister back. The sister who loved being alive and being around people is coming out of her shell for a visit as we are watching and is changing her life. It may be hard to accept what she does at times, but it has been years since she tried to be happy and loving and we will have to be patient as she remembers how to do it. She did not mean to hurt you for all those years but now she realizes that she did. Neither you or she can go back and change what has happened but you both can forgive one another and go on with your lives together."

Homer dismally said, "I can see how she has done some of those things and I can also see that she is trying to change. I know that she did not like how she was in the past. I guess I should go home and try to speak to her now."

Homer just turned on his heels and went toward the house. He hesitated at the door but continued inside. He found his mother in her favorite chair rocking and humming. He could see the red puffy eyes that had shed many tears since his words last night. He walked into the room silently and then he spoke as she looked up at his coming in. He said, "I'm sorry momma. I know that I hurt you last night with what I said when I was angry. I was not expecting what would happen and I did not have time to straighten it out in my mind for a while. I am not angry anymore and I am sorry for what I said."

His momma did not say anything for a few minutes as she looked for words within herself. She looked away as she said, "You spoke in truth last night about how things have been. I was so angry all those years and wanted to be alone after your pa died. I had no right as your mother to keep you as isolated as I did for all those years. It is not that I meant to keep a secret about your Uncle Stanley. It is just the fact that I did not want to be around anyone. They are the only known living relatives other than your Uncle Jake that we have, and I never so much as gave them the time of day for over fifteen years. I have been praying to Jesus to help me become less bitter toward people and He made it noticeably clear to me that the healing would have to be started by me. That is when I wrote them a letter and asked for forgiveness for all those years. I guess I should have started a little closer to home with the forgiveness part. I used you as an excuse to be angry at your father in the strangest kind of way. We both had wanted children and we both loved you when you were born. Your pa would get down on the floor and play with you for hours when he could. I would have to get after him to do the things that needed to be done around the house instead of playing with you. He stayed home a couple of days from work after he got hurt and played with you instead of going to the doctors and having his leg looked at. That is how I got the twisted idea in my head that it was your fault that he died and now I would have to take care of you alone. You were not to blame for your pa's death, but you were right here in the house for me to blame for all those years. It was even worse when we lost the house to the bank, and I refused to move into the house as Jake wanted me to. My parents knew that if I had to keep things going on the farm that I would lose it to the bank as well. I knew that deep in my heart, but I would not take Jake's help and accused him of feeling sorry for me instead of keeping a promise to our parents about helping me as much as he could. I have been a very spiteful woman for a long time, and I don't even like me so how could you."

Homer said, "There have been times when I have not liked you such as last night, but you are my momma and that is all that matters to me. I forgive you for the times we have had, and I hope I never speak up in anger again. I like the new you and things are getting better for us. I should have my car on the road very soon and maybe we can drive over and see their home as well someday."

His momma smiled up at him from her chair and asked him if he was hungry.

Chapter Eight

Homer was adding some fresh shavings to the chicken coop, so the floor would be warmer for the chickens. The egg laying was at its prime and they were getting an egg a day per chicken. They were medium to large eggs of a rosy-brown color and an occasional speck of black on the shell. They bring eggs to the store twice a week now. Homer was surprised that the chickens did not eat any more mash than when they were just growing now that they were laying eggs. He was going to kill a couple of the white leghorns today for his uncle and them. They had grown to be about a ten-pound bird when dressed. You had to use a roasting pan to bake them in or you had to cut them into smaller pieces. His uncle had the red heifer slaughtered about a week ago and they were going to get the meat today.

Homer decided that it would be a nice day to take his gun and go for a walk in the woods. They did not need the meat as badly, but a fresh rabbit was still good to eat occasionally. Homer had gotten a book on how to raise rabbits as he had wanted to in the past and the idea was still on his mind. The biggest thing was where to find some breed able rabbit does that he could buy to start with. He had taken a few boards from a shipping crate from the garage and had started making nests from the boards and the wire that he had gotten from the farmer. The book said that you only needed one buck rabbit for several does if you spaced the breeding apart and that also helped you have rabbits ready to eat at given intervals. They needed a brooding box and an exercise area that could be raised wire suspended off the ground. A litter was ready in six to eight weeks for slaughtering. The book said that some restaurants would buy rabbit meat for their menus. He was remembering all this as he walked along the edge of the field in search of a meal. He was inching along as quietly as he could as he kept in the shadows of the trees. He was nearing his uncle's pond when he heard some noise from that direction. He looked ahead and could see some migrating ducks that were late for the year carrying on at the pond. He moved into the tree line and approached the birds unnoticed. He would have a reasonable shot if he could take another three steps without them seeing him. He readied his shotgun and made the final approach to the ducks. He could already see that they were mallards and he set his sight on a big drake and fired. Water sprayed all around the drake from the shotgun blast, but he was dead in the water. Homer tried to get another shell in the gun before the others flew off, but he was too slow. One duck was better than no ducks he thought to himself. He went to the shore of the pond and could see that he needed a pole or something to get the drake to shore now that he had shot it. If it had been summer, he would have taken his clothes off and gone in to get the bird. He looked at the edge of the woods and found a pole that he thought would be long enough to do what he had to do. It took a couple of tries from a couple of positions, but he finally had the drake on the shore. This would be enough meat for today and he started back home with his prize. He could pluck it at the same time as he did the two chickens that he was supposed to kill today.

Homer had gotten his driver's license today and he was strutting around the garage like a rooster. His car was ready to go on the road and things were going to be different again. His uncle had told him that he would now be getting a key to the garage, and he was going to be responsible for opening it in the morning sometimes. The other mechanic did not do that, so Homer was starting to sense the trust that his uncle was putting in him now. He was also being taught how to charge for the work that they did in case his uncle was not around and a customer wanted to pay and leave with their car. The work of changing a tire was easy because the price did not change but the costs of new tires had to be addressed differently. His uncle had a price sheet on the wall if the customer had not gotten a quote from his uncle and had it written on the work order beforehand. All this was quite amazing from the young man who had started to work there only a few months ago when he could not read yet.

Homer and his momma had been getting along better as of late. She took the time to tell Homer some stories of his pa and her from years past and included his Uncle Stanley in some of them. She had even laughed at the telling of some of them if they were special in her memory. They were talking one night, and she told of a special event in which his pa had taken her on a special trip by train. At the end of the story, she made a comment on how she had not remembered that trip for years with a tear in her eye. There was one night when they were with Jake and Flora and she and Jake joined in telling the story about their childhood on the farm. They told of the work on the farm but also how their parents had special times of the year that they would spend with them. The county fair was the highlight for the two of them and how their mother had won pie baking contests for years. It was during those fairs that brother and sister met their future mates. It became a special night for the two of them in playing its part in the healing of Sis and her anger toward Jake.

Homer had finished four nesting boxes to hold rabbits that he was going to raise. He had met someone at the garage that told him of where there were some rabbits for sale. They belonged to a young man who was going to be going into the military and he did not want to leave them for his mother to care for while he was gone. In the discussing of the price for the rabbits, the young man gave Homer many important pointers about how to keep his rabbits healthy and producing. He explained how to improve the chances of multiple births by leaving the buck and the doe together a little longer but not too long. He told Homer how to choose young doe rabbits from the litter to keep them from getting too old as breeding stock. He also gave the name of a couple of restaurants that he had sold meat to at different times. Homer listened and took notes about their care. At the end of the talk, Homer had bought all the rabbits that were not ready to eat and two free standing cages to add to his four. The young man had a friend with a truck, and everything was taken to the farm for Homer.

Jake and Homer were at the garage one day, when a customer came back to complain about some work that had been done at the garage. The man was yelling and carrying on about how some damage had happened to his car while it was in the garage. Homer had done the work and he was speaking softly to the man despite the yelling. Homer asked to see the damage and the man took him out and showed him a dent behind the passenger's door. It was deeper on one end than the other and had some rust beginning in the dent. Homer simply asked the man what made him think that it had happened in the garage. The man yelled that he had been the only one near the car recently. Homer made the simple statement that he had not worked on that side of the car at all and that the dent was older than a couple of days old with the rust in it. Homer also asked him if anyone else was driving his car recently. The man replied that he had lent the car to his nephew, but he had not reported any damage to him. Homer asked the man if he had asked his nephew about the damage before he had come back to the station. The man simply said no as he left the garage still yelling at them both. Jake simply looked at Homer as it ended and said, "I don't know how you kept your temper so well but that was a good job of handling that customer. Thank you!"

Later that same day, the man was back to the garage, and

he had a look of shame on his face. He said, "I came back to see you two because I wasn't very much of a man in the way that I yelled at you. I did get my nephew to tell me how he had hit a piece of equipment on a farm one day and he did not want to tell me about it. I don't know why you did not get angry at me earlier today, but I am sorry for accusing you and yelling at you."

Homer said, "There wasn't much of a reason to get mad at you because I knew that I did not do the damage to your car. You might never have found out the truth if I had gotten mad and yelled back at you. I am glad that you now know and there are no hard feelings as far as we are concerned. I do think more of you for having come back though. Thank you."

The man left in a couple of minutes and Jake said, "I know that you have seen enough anger in your life for a lifetime already, but you surely showed some wisdom in the way you spoke to that customer today. I am proud to have you working for me."

Homer did not change expressions as he said, "Thanks for saying that but I don't feel that I did anything special in not getting mad at a mad person. Look how many years and how many lives momma wasted and troubled and all it got her was misery and a lot of years of loneliness for herself. Life is better now that she is no longer angry with everyone in the world."

Jake agreed and said, "It surely is at that," and they both went back to work.

Homer was sitting in the living room reading a book that he had gotten from his uncle's library. His momma was in the kitchen working on some biscuits to go with the stewed chicken she had for tonight. It was a story of Moses leading his people out of Egypt and explained parts that were not in the bible including a lot of facts about the culture of the times. He had read a couple of chapters by the time that his momma came in to sit down for a while. They started talking about the many miracles that God performed to convince Pharaoh to release the Israelites. His momma told of having seen parts of the American desert when she had gone on that train ride so many years ago. She said that she had been told that the desert in Egypt was hotter and was nearly all sand that changed shapes by the blowing of the winds across the area. Homer asked her if she believed in the miracles that God had done for them in the desert. She told him that she had no reason to not believe the stories from the bible and how most of them had been proven to be true over time. She also said that she believed in miracles every time she saw a child born. Homer asked her what she meant. She replied that the bible spoke of God creating all life known on the earth and she felt that He was still at work when a man and a woman could help Him by having a baby and bringing a new life into the world. She then asked him if he was ready to eat because the meal was ready.

Homer was at the service station the next day and the other mechanic had to go and get some parts for the car that he was working on. His uncle was at the bank, so Homer had to pump gas as well as work on the car in the shop. He heard a customer pull up by the pumps and went out to pump the gas for them. He walked up to the window of the driver and asked him what he needed. There was a young man in the car that looked vaguely familiar to him, but he was not sure until the man spoke.

The man said, "Well, if it isn't Homer the big dummy pumping gas for his uncle."

The man was saying it for the benefit of the people he had riding with him, and Homer just looked in the window at the man he now recognized as Jimmy Taylor from town. They had gone to school together for a short time years ago, but Homer had not seen him for a long time. Now he was in the car making fun of him like he had so many years ago and the other people were laughing with him. Homer had never seen him come here for gas before because he would have recognized the new car. Homer repeated his question and ignored Jimmy and his friends. Jimmy asked to have his gas tank filled up and the oil checked and started to comment about whether Homer could find the hood on the car to his friends. Homer started the gas pumping and went to open the hood as he had been asked. He removed the oil dipstick and found it to be full and he knew that the new car was not using oil, but Jimmy had wanted to humiliate him in front of his friends. As he replaced the dipstick, Homer happened to pull a spark plug wire off from the front cylinder of Jimmy's car. He then put it back as if it were all the way on the plug as it should be. He then closed the hood and finished pumping the gas. Homer asked for the twelve dollars and sixty cents from Jimmy, and he was handed a twenty-dollar bill. He then went inside to get the correct change and brought it back out to him. Jimmy made a few parting comments for his friends to hear as he left, but Homer just walked back to the garage with a hidden smile on his face.

Homer was at the shed trying to see the first litter of rabbits that had been born the other day. He had not been able to count how many the doe had in the litter, and he was trying to see. He had bred a second doe the following week, so he was expecting her to litter right off also. He brushed the doe from her nest and found five little rabbits concealed by her. He let her come right back to them as it was still chilly in the early mornings now. It was nearing the time to order more chickens meant for eating and in a month or, so he would order some new laying chicks as well. He and his uncle had traded some eating chickens for a couple of new calves from a farmer who had his work done at the garage so there were not many of them left. He knew that the egg production would be going down drastically within a couple of months, and they would start to eat those chickens as well. Homer and his momma felt that it was time to buy a freezer for keeping some of the meat that they were processing. They bought a chest style freezer from a catalog and had it shipped to the house and placed it on the porch. It was going to be helpful to their increased needs now.

Homer's momma was staying busier than she used to. She would have Homer drive her to town occasionally and she had bought some pots and soil to start some plants in the house that they were going to put in the garden. She was still visiting the neighbor and their children during the day while he was at work. She had brought home some of the woman's mending to help her keep up with her families' needs. The farmer was going to come back this spring and till the garden loose one more time in return for the help.

Homer and his momma had discovered that they both liked long grained brown rice with some of their meals. Now that his momma could plan on what was going into the pot on any given day, she could be more creative with her meals. Flora had taught her how to make some delicious casseroles baked with rice and flavored to the meat that was in it. His momma had even put on a few pounds of weight with the new diet and her face looked more pleasant. They were looking in cookbooks for more ways to fix rabbit as a meal.

The man who sold him the rabbits had given him a couple of names to restaurants that would buy the meat from him, and he was going to contact them as he got some meat ready. They even had said that they would buy the kidneys and liver by the pound if he accumulated them during the slaughter of the rabbits. That was one more reason to have the new freezer on the porch. The one thing that they had both insisted on was that the rabbits be fed only alfalfa pellets that had been processed for them and Homer was using that feed now.

Homer was at work again later in the week and he heard a commotion out by the gas pumps. He recognized the new car and the voice of the man who was yelling at his uncle and asking him where the dummy was. His uncle was not sure who he was asking about and had to ask Jimmy Taylor who he was speaking about. He cussed again and called out for Homer. Homer gave it a minute of thought and then went out to speak to Jimmy.

Homer walked out and said, "Hello Jimmy. I am glad to see that you are becoming a regular customer."

Jimmy let out a string of profanities and told Homer that he was going to get even with him for what he had done to his car.

Homer kept a straight face and replied, "I don't have any idea what you are yelling about but if you care to explain we will try to fix it. All I did was gas your car with our high-quality gasoline and check your oil. What do you think that I did to your car during that time?"

Jimmy cussed again and said, "You know very well that you pulled one of my spark-plug wires and then set it back in place without its making contact. It cost me twenty dollars to have a mechanic at the dealership find the problem. You are going to pay me back for that work with gasoline until I get my money back."

Homer snapped back, "I don't know what makes you think

that a dummy like me would know how to do that but if you leave today without paying for your gas, we will have you charged with theft. It was nice seeing you again."

Homer turned and went back into the garage and left Jimmy cussing at his uncle, but he paid for his gas before leaving. When his uncle came to see him, he said, "Do you think he will really become a steady customer from now on? I think I know what happened, but I suggest you don't do anything else to his car if he comes back." Homer just nodded to his uncle as he went back to work.

Chapter Nine

It was Saturday morning and Homer, and his momma were going to town to get some baking things. As they drove along, Homer spotted Pastor Murray standing beside his car with the hood up. They pulled over to the side of the road and asked him if he had a problem. He told Homer that it had sputtered a couple of times and then just stopped running. Homer told him that he did not have many tools with him, but he would have a look and see if he could find the problem. It was just a couple of minutes of looking at the engine and he spotted the problem. The pastor had gotten an accumulation of water somewhere in his gas and the fuel filter was plugged. Homer said he could try to drain it there or he could go and get a new one from the garage. They opted for the new one, so they got in Homer's car to go and get one. Pastor Mike thanked him for stopping and helping him out. He then made a comment about not knowing that Homer could drive a car.

Homer smiled as he replied, "It was less than a year ago that I learned to read at all. My uncle had a teacher stop at the garage a couple of times per week and she gave me private lessons and then my momma started helping me. I worked for my uncle every day and finally got enough money to buy a car and get my license. Uncle Jake encouraged me a great deal by telling me that I was not stupid but unlearned. I am now a mechanic at his shop, and we keep chickens and rabbits at home for meat. Momma tends the garden in the summer, and we are getting along better than any time prior in my life. Now I will go in here and get a couple of my tools and a new filter for your car."

Homer was only inside for a few minutes and returned with a pouch of items that he might need on the side of the road. They continued the small talk as they returned to Pastor Murray's car. Pastor said, "You could not read a few months ago. I think your uncle is an incredibly wise man in helping you. You could get almost any job now you can read but I imagine that you enjoy what you are so good at."

Homer said, "I do like what I do even if it is hard and dirty. I have never thought about getting another job and I am not interested in one. Some people still think I am stupid, but I do not have a problem ignoring them. Let them think what they want because it does not change how good things are going for my momma and me. I should have this changed in just a few minutes and you can be on your way."

Homer worked on the car for just a few minutes and then told Pastor Mike that he did not owe him anything for what he had done. He tried to insist but Homer told him to just thank Jesus for sending someone to help him when he needed it the most. Homer waited until Pastor Mike was safely on the road and then they continued their way to the store.

Homer asked his uncle if they could put some meat birds in

his coop again and he felt that it had been a very worthwhile project. Homer agreed to kill the last of the big birds and clean the coop before the new chicks arrived in about a week.

Homer was working at the station every day and he noticed a young woman who came in and got gas from them. He would frequently try to pump her gas himself and tried to speak to her about different things while he was out there. He finally got up enough nerve to ask her name one day. She told him her name was Alice and asked him his name. Homer told her his name and then had to end the conversation as she was pulling away. It was very unusual for a young woman to not shy away from him if they knew him, so Homer found this very refreshing and quite stimulating. One day as he walked back into the station to place the money into the register, his uncle asked him if he was ever going to ask her to go out with him. Homer could feel his face turn red and asked his uncle what he meant by the comment. His uncle said, "What I mean is that it is all right for you to like someone of the opposite sex. You might see if you could take her out for some coffee or ice cream and see what it is like to be with her."

Homer blurted out, "I have never been around any girls or women except momma and Aunt Flora. I know that I think she is pretty, but I would not know how to act around her. The only thing I know well is my work and my animals."

The conversation only lasted a few more minutes, but his uncle told him that they could talk after work if he wanted. Then his uncle asked him a question that he was not expecting. Jake asked, “Are you interested in learning how to run this station and maybe buying it in the future? I am not going to live forever, and I would like it if it stayed in the family. Your grandfather started this business as a young man, and I learned it from him. You have a natural knack for the work, and I believe that you could learn the paperwork if you wanted to. It would take some time, but I believe that it would be a good thing.”

Homer’s face lit up like a light bulb at the questions. He said, “I have never thought of not working for you since I started. I guess I never gave your age any thought before today. If you are serious, I would love to do that with you.”

They agreed to speak about it again later, but it was agreed that Homer was going to learn the paperwork as quickly as possible. Then Homer had to ask, “Are you feeling poorly?”

Jake answered, “I have a few aches and pains that all older folks have but as far as I know I am healthy. I just want some time to spend with your aunt that is not on the farm or in this garage. We have managed to save some money from running this garage and you will probably have to care for the entire farm at our death. I know how your mother thinks charity is why I have done this, but I have made money from the work you have done for me, and I want to leave the farm and the business in the family. The judge and his family do not want for money and your aunt, and I have already agreed on what to do with it at the time of our death. Now please finish the work we have for today."

Homer was delivering the first rabbit meat that the restaurants had ordered from him. It was not a large order, but it was the beginning of a new enterprise for him. He had already decided that if this went well that he was going to build some more nesting crates and start a few more breeding does in the shed. Homer wanted the animals to pay for the things they needed for the house, so the garage could pay for itself more easily. His momma was starting to take an interest in caring for the animals and Homer merely had to do the slaughtering of them. The two calves that they had gotten from the farmer were in their pen and had been weaned from the milk supplement to grain.

Homer was busy at the garage learning how to do estimates on the sale of tires and improving his skills with numbers in general. His uncle had taken an entire week and traveled to another state with his aunt and things had gone very well while he was gone. The checking account was having times of confusion with him, but he kept on learning as time went by. What was going well at the garage was seeing Alice. He had taken her out for coffee a couple of times and this Sunday he was going to go and have a picnic with her near a lake. He was looking forward to that. He was thinking of her as he drove to the restaurant. Homer was speaking to the owner and asking him how much rabbit meat he wanted delivered and how often. They laid out a proposal to start with and then they shook hands on the deal. Homer was to bring eight fresh rabbits weighing around two pounds every two weeks to begin with. Homer left pleased with the arrangements but knew that he was going to have to find some more markets for his rabbits as well. The other thing that Homer was trying to find out about was selling furs from the backs of the rabbits to a fur trader. He had heard that he might be able to sell them for almost a dollar a piece and that would more than pay for the alfalfa it took to raise them.

Homer and Alice were driving to the lake on Sunday with a basket of food and drinks in the back seat. They had a blanket to place on the ground and this was going to be fun. Alice was sitting in the middle of the seat right next to Homer. She was in a flowery dress with her hair done nicely and with a light fragrance of lilac perfume emanating from her. Homer was feeling as bold as he ever had in his life as he began to speak to her. He said, "I would like to tell you something if you promise not to laugh at me."

Alice looked at him and could see that he was very somber and said, "What would that be Homer, and I promise not to laugh."

Homer said, "You are the first woman that I have ever been near other than my momma. I did not go to school, so I was never around people of my own age, and I am not sure how to do things with you and not hurt you in any way."

Alice looked at him intently and asked, "You never went to school at all when you were younger? You seem to be doing all right now. Tell me some of what has happened to you."

Homer looked at her again before he began, "I have never spoken about this to anyone and for years I did not know that life could be different than what I knew with my momma. I do not remember my father who died when I was young. My momma became terribly angry at the world, and we lived alone in our house until the bank took it away from her. Uncle Jake tried to have her move into the house where we live now but she refused, and we lived in a tar paper shack on my grandfather's farm until I was twenty years old. I was two years older than any of the other kids when my momma finally sent me to school. I had never been around people, and I was always in trouble, and I became labeled as a dummy before I quit school altogether within a couple of months of starting. I do not remember having any toys or anything else in the house as I grew up. It was just my momma and me. I learned to hunt and fish so that we could have some meat on the table, but it was never good at home. One day a town health officer told us that we could not stay in the shack anymore because it did not have a toilet. This was the last straw with my momma, so she burned the shack down that day, and we had nothing. That was when we moved into the house on the farm, and I started working for my uncle at the garage. He was a great influence in my life as he told me that I was not stupid but merely unlearned."

Alice sat quietly beside him as he continued to tell of his life. He said, "I was working one day when my uncle had a teacher stop by the garage and start to teach me how to read. My uncle says

I learned so well because I was ready for my life to be different, and that hunger made me work hard. I learned to read well enough to pass my driving license and bought this car from a customer. I have never stopped working for my uncle and that gave me the chance to meet you. I have had to learn about life away from my momma for the most part, but this is totally new to me. I spent years of my life content to be alone but that is no longer true. I do not know how to tell you how much I like you and want to spend time with you without telling you what I have just said. I guess I need to know if you are willing to teach me how to be your friend or maybe even more as time goes by."

Alice sat there for a few minutes in silence and just put her hand on his. She finally said, "I have never met anyone like you before. You have made it so easy for me to like you or to hurt you by what you have said. I could be like so many people who have made fun of you because of what you do not know but I have liked you ever since I met you. I have spent my last two dollars on gas, so I could go by and see you at work. You are the first man who has been as innocent in so many ways around me. I mean that in a flattering way."

Homer said, "What does the word flattering mean?"

Alice smiled and answered, "It means to compliment someone with words. You have never said one crude word to me, and you do not seem to speak of your life in anger when you have a right to be angry. You have not made fun of my looks or anything else about me like, so many mean people have said and done during our lives."

Homer flatly stated, "My momma was the angriest person I have ever met. I saw her wither up and almost die in her anger. It is better for us now, but I have no time to be angry with how people think or feel about me. I had a boy who knew me come by this winter and stop at the station and start to make fun of me, so his friends would laugh. I do not have time to be angry about people like that. I guess that is why I like my animals so much. We just exist together in a world that has no anger, even when I slaughter them for food."

They had reached the lake now and they got their food and drinks and put them on the blanket on the shore. Homer was sitting down on the blanket next to Alice when a big smile came over his face. He looked at her and said, "It wasn't that long ago that someone finally told me that men and women don't swim together without any clothes on. A neighbor's daughter and I had been swimming in the same pond for years and one day she decided that she did not want me to look at her naked anymore. I had to go home and find out what she was mad about."

Alice was laughing at him by this time. She said, "You have always gone swimming in the nude in the past."

Homer started to be offended as he said, "I used to go to a neighbor's pond to bathe and get cooled down and I never put on clothes to go in the water. It seemed to spoil the purpose of wanting to be clean and free while in the water. In the past, I would not have liked you laughing at me for that story, but I can see the humor in it myself now. I really do not know how to be around a woman such as yourself and I want to be around you."

Alice blushed as she said, "Well, it is a little too early in our relationship for you to go swimming in the nude with me. Maybe in a little while it will be more fun to do it together."

She was still smiling as Homer said, "I would like to know something about your life and what you like to do."

Alice took a deep breath and answered, "I won't bore you with much of my life. I am one of three children my parents had, and I am in the middle. I have never been strong and never played sports, but I loved to read. I like to read about all the places that this big world can offer. I believe that I would love to sail on the ocean one day and watch the sun go down on the horizon. I also would like to be on a mountain top and watch the sun rise to me first before it shows itself to anyone else below. I guess you would have to call me a romanticist and a bit of a bookworm. That is why I work at a library."

They ate what they had brought for a picnic lunch and picked up the dishes and put them back into the basket. Alice was the first to take Homer by the hand and ask him to walk with her along the shore of the lake. They walked and talked for a long time enjoying the scenery around them and watching frogs jump into the water for safety as they neared. They watched a fat old porcupine amble along the shore to get a drink and then return to the safety of the woods. At one point, the wind was causing little ripples that were reflecting the sunlight onto the trees around them and making the leaves shimmer and shine. They walked to the point of a dead tree stopping their progress and then decided it was time to go home. They returned along the shore hand in hand and looking at each other as they went. Homer opened the door for her at the car and she slid into the middle of the seat. They sat by each other as they drove along, and Alice thanked him for such a lovely time.

Homer confidently added, "I would like to do this or something different with you again next week if you would let me. I had a really good time, and I am glad that you accepted my invitation to invite you on a picnic. I must deliver some rabbit meat to a restaurant next weekend, but I could pick you up after that. You could even go with me if you wanted to, but I must do my work first. I am trying to sell enough meat to pay for the needs of the house, so I can buy the garage from my uncle when it is time. I guess I am trying to make up for lost time in some way. I just want to have a life that is not filled with anger or needs because you do not have anything. I want those days to be done."

Alice stated, "Those are honorable and reasonable requests to make for your life. I admire the fact that you have a plan now and you are following it the best you can. I do not hear you saying that you want to be rich, but I understand the part about needing the basic things in life occasionally. We have gone through that as a family, and it can make people angry. It doesn't sound as if we had it quite as bad as you did but I know what you mean."

Homer changed the pitch of his voice as he said, "If that is pity you are feeling for me, you better stop it right now. Life is what it is, and you can change some things, but you cannot change all things. You cannot change the things that have happened in the past and I would not want to. It has made me who I am and showed me what I do not want to be if I can help it."

Alice said in a sheepish voice, "I wasn't feeling pity for you Homer. You have reminded me of some things in my past that I would like to forget but that would not change it for me either. I like the way you view your life now and I hope that I get a chance to share at least a small part of it. I would love to go with you when you take your meat to the market next week. Should we pack a lunch with us again?"

They finished making their plans as they arrived at Alice's house. They were going to see each other one more time at the garage this week and set a time to leave on Saturday. Homer got out and opened the car door for her to get out and took a couple of steps with her as she turned toward her house. She stopped and kissed him on the cheek and told him she would see him this week sometime. Homer stood there stunned for a moment and then he got into his car and headed home.

Homer's Shack

Chapter Ten

Homer got home from his time with Alice and busied himself around the sheds and the chickens. He knew that his momma was going to ask him all about his day and he wanted to cherish it a little longer before being asked about it. He cleaned and leveled his uncle's coop to get it ready for the chicks arriving on Monday. He was thinking that he would have to ask the farmer to let him use the equipment to spread the cleaning in the fields. They had a mixed pile of heifer, chicken, and rabbit dung accumulating and needing to be spread. He prepared the feeder and the chick water pan and went to check on his new arrival of rabbits.

He finally went into the house and found his momma in her room, so he just went upstairs to his. She would call him for supper when it was time. He started to read his latest book about raising rabbits and how to market the meat in his area. This book had what appeared to be overly complicated pens for their rabbits and Homer did not understand why they had it that hard to do something so simple. He read for a while and noticed that he had not heard his momma moving around yet. He went downstairs and called her name at the door to her room. He called again when she did not answer him. He then knocked on the door and called out louder and he thought that he had heard a moan coming from her room. He cracked the door open and saw that she was lying on top of her bed, but she did not respond to him. He went to the bed and touched her, and she was limp in his hands but warm. He knew that it was time to get some help and he ran to his uncle's house calling out his name.

Jake was sitting in their living room after having eaten and thought that he heard Homer calling his name. He could not understand why that was happening until he heard it again and louder this time. He got up from his chair and Flora looked in from the kitchen as Homer threw open their door.

Homer screamed, "I can't wake my momma up. I cannot wake my momma up. She just moaned one time, but she is not moving at all."

By this time, the three of them were on their way to the other house. Homer beat them to the house and went right into his momma's room and spoke to her again with the same results. Flora went to the other side of the bed and started to examine his momma as she lay there. Jake stood at the end of the bed trying to formulate a plan without knowing what the need really was, but he was thinking it would require a ride to the hospital in the next town. Flora finally spoke and said, "This looks like a stroke, and she will have to go to the hospital right away. Jake, you get our car, and I will help Homer carry her out to the car."

Everyone started doing their part of the plan decided upon by Flora. Homer went to pick her up and stated that she had wet herself. Flora told him to take a different blanket and they would put it under her in the car to help keep her warm from the moisture. It was not easy to get a limp person into the back seat of a car, but they managed it and headed down the road as quickly as they dared. Homer sat in the back seat with her head in his lap and kept her from being thrown around during the ride.

They arrived at the hospital and Flora told Homer to wait and they would get some way to help carry her into the hospital. A nurse came out with Jake and Flora, and they had a gurney to lay Sis down on. Homer came around to the side of the car and helped to lift his momma out and onto the gurney. It was as difficult to get her out as it had been to get her into the car. The nurse told them to lift on the blanket they had put on the seat instead of lifting on her to keep from injuring her. With that advice, they got her lifted and, on the gurney, and headed for the door. The nurse had them stop at a desk and give another nurse as much information as they could, and they would get her into an examination room. Homer was having problems concentrating on anything they asked so Jake took over.

Jake informed the nurse, "Her name is Molly Baker, but everyone calls her Sis. She is currently forty-eight years old and was born on July seventh. She is widowed and lives with her son Homer on our farm. All we know is that she was in her room when Homer came in from going to town and he did not check on her until later. That is when he found her unresponsive on her bed and has only moaned one time in the hour that it took to get her into the car and get her here."

The nurse decidedly said, "That is enough information for now and we will have her examined by the doctor and we will come and find you if you would wait in the room you see right over there."

Jake and Flora had to prompt Homer to come into the room and wait for the doctor to come out. He would not sit down for the longest time and just kept pacing the floor and looking at the door. It seemed like forever, but the doctor came out in about twenty minutes.

The doctor stood looking at them and said, "I believe that you folks had already guessed that Sis has had a serious stroke and is not responding now. We have given her a medication to lower her blood pressure as quickly as possible, but she is not responding to that yet. We can give her some more if she does not respond soon. This is going to be an exceedingly long night for her, and the next few days will tell us a lot of what you can expect in the future. Is there anything else you want to tell me regarding Sis or her care?

Jake hesitantly said, "Our mother died of a stroke, but she was twenty years older than Sis at the time. She has not had any kind of medical history since she had Homer twenty-one years ago."

"That information is helpful, and I must tell you that Sis could have the same outcome," the doctor said. "There is nothing we can do for Sis that isn't being done to keep that from happening. I would like you all to go home and get some rest. I know that will not be easy, but I would like you to come back tomorrow evening and we will try to let you see her at that time. Is there a way to contact you if I need to find you any sooner?"

They gave the doctor the two telephone numbers for their house and the garage as well. Homer asked if he could stay with her, and the doctor assured him that it would be best to come back tomorrow. He wanted to argue but his uncle encouraged him to do as the doctor had said. It was a long drive home from the hospital and Jake asked Homer if he was going to be okay alone. He told them he would be fine, and he would see his uncle at the station in the morning. He reminded his uncle that they were expecting the chicks tomorrow also.

Homer let himself into the dark house and studied what he would have to do to keep things going. He would get up early and pick the eggs and feed the rabbits that his momma had been helping to do during the day. He could not go into his momma's room, but he knew that he would have to clean her bed and make it fresh before she came home. He did not feel hungry, but he thought that it would be better if he ate something tonight and help his stomach to settle down. He suddenly thought of Alice and wondered if she could be helpful in helping keep his mind busy or if she would be annoyed at the request. He made himself a sandwich from some left-over chicken in the refrigerator and then went to his room for the night.

Homer woke up early after a fitful night of sleep where he thought he heard his mother calling him from her room. He wondered if she had tried to call him, and he had not heard her. He did the animal chores quickly and went to the garage early. He had a brake job that he had not finished on Friday and dove right into that. He sold gas to two customers before anyone else got to the garage but neither one was Alice. He might try to find her at the library during lunchtime. Jake got there a little later than usual and Homer asked him if the doctor had called. Jake said no and that they could go over together tonight so they could see her.

Homer did go to the library during the noon break. He had never been in the building, so he had to look around to find anyone. He found Alice putting books back on the shelf from a cart that she was pushing around. She smiled and gave a friendly hello as Homer walked over to her. Homer was too nervous to beat around the bush and said, "When I got home from being with you yesterday, I did some chores with the animals before going into the house. When I went in, momma was in her room, and I did not disturb her at the time. I came down from my room in the dark and found her unconscious on her bed. We took her to the hospital, and she has had a severe stroke and may die."

Alice came right over to Homer and cuddled up against his chest and held him for a couple of minutes. She finally looked up and said, "Homer, I am so sorry. Are you going to see her today?"

"We are going over tonight, and they might let us see her in her room," Homer said. "They were trying to get her blood pressure down with medicine last night and they would not let us stay. I just had to come and see you with this bad news. I need someone to talk to before I explode."

Alice tenderly said, "I am so glad that you feel that you can come and see me. I will go with you tonight if you want me to. I can come right over after work, and we can all go."

Homer let his arms go around her and held on tighter than he realized, and she let out a moan. He said, "I'm so sorry. I did not mean to hurt you. I do think that I could explode if I am not careful. Would you really come with me tonight?"

Alice simply said, "I will call my parents and tell them what is going on and I will come over around three o'clock when my replacement comes in. Do not worry any more than you must because I believe that it will be okay. You just wait and see."

To add to the confusion, the new chicks got there around two-thirty in the afternoon. Homer had told his uncle that Alice was going to go over with them, and he said that would be fine. Alice got there a few minutes after three and Jake asked them to take the chicks to the farm and he would close the garage a little early and be home a little after four. Alice followed him to the farm in her car. Homer took the little chicks into the coop as Alice watched from outside and let them out of the box. He showed a couple of them where the mash was, a couple more where the water was, and then locked them in. Homer led Alice into the house by the hand and said, "Thank you for going with me. You don't have to do this."

Alice assured him that she wanted to go. Homer took a couple of minutes to go and check the rabbits and pick up any more eggs from the daytime. He then went in and noticed that his momma's bed was made up nice and fresh. He offered Alice a seat as he went upstairs to get out of his coveralls that he had not changed out of today while at the station. He told her that there might be some iced tea in the refrigerator if she wanted to help herself. She had poured two glasses by the time he got back downstairs. She offered one to him and told him it was going to work out.

They arrived at the hospital just before dark and went to the visitor entrance. They asked where Molly Baker's room was and were sent upstairs and directed to another reception area. That nurse said that she would have the nurse who was caring for her come out and speak to them. They waited in the hall and Alice held Homer's hand very tightly. Homer had introduced Alice to his aunt and uncle on the way over and it turned out that they knew her parents. The nurse arrived and took them into a room that was empty, so they could speak in private.

The nurse began, "This is usually done by the doctor, but he is in an emergency on the first floor now. I can only tell you what anyone can tell by seeing her and cannot tell you what is going to happen so please do not ask. She has responded quite well to the medication to drop her blood pressure during the first twenty-four hours. We are seeing some movement on her right side, and we hope that she was right-handed before this. She seems to feel nothing on her left side currently. She has opened her eyes a couple of times, but we cannot tell if she is hearing us. She may recognize you as her family or she may not, but it is too early to know what to expect. The human body needs a long time to recover from a stroke as severe as she has had. Why don't I take you into her room and I will try to get the message to the doctor that you have arrived."

They followed the nurse to a room a little farther down the hall and she stopped one more time at the door. She allowed the four of them to go in first and position themselves around the bed and she stayed at the foot of the bed. Sis had some fluids being given to her by intravenous and she had some pillows propping her up on her left side. The nurse began again, "You may touch her but be careful of the tubes. Most doctors believe that stroke patients can hear but cannot respond. Please speak to her as honestly as you would like to but be encouraging with your words. I will give you some time alone, but you can push the button on the wall if you need me and I will come right away." She then turned and walked out of the room.

Homer looked at his momma lying as still as she had been

yesterday. She was warm to the touch, but she was paler that she normally was. Homer bent over her and whispered loudly into the ear about missing her. Then he tried to introduce her to Alice and tell her who she was. There was not the slightest movement or change of expression on her face as he spoke. Alice did say hello to her from where she stood beside Homer holding his hand. Jake and Flora also went up to the bed and spoke to her and rubbed her on the shoulder that was up in the bed. They continued to gently speak to her occasionally as they watched her lying without motion. They were so intent on what they were doing that they did not hear the doctor come to the room until he knocked on the door to get their attention.

The doctor started, "Good evening, folks. We have had a positive twenty-four hours around here. Sis has responded to the medication that we put her on and her blood pressure has been stable but a little higher than normal for the last six hours. We will continue with the medication for another couple of days to be on the safe side. She has been seen to have some movement on her right side and she does respond to stimuli on that side. She does not have any response on the left side. The immediate danger to her life seems to be over but she will need a long time to recover from this and if she ever does heal completely, it would be a miracle. You will have a long time to make plans for her coming home but life for her and you will not be the same. We can wait a few more days and talk about this again so you can get ready. I suggest you try to go about your life in the daytime as close to normal as you can and visit her at night for a while. Do you have any questions that do not ask me to make any guesses or promises now?"

None of them had any questions that made any sense, so they were all quiet. The doctor asked them to not stay too long, and he would see them again soon as he left the room. The four of them said their good nights to Sis and they left her there as they went home. Jake and Flora heard Homer say to Alice that he was going to ask Jesus to make his momma well again and they just looked at each other.

They arrived home and the four of them went to the two houses. Alice was still holding Homer's hand most of the time as she followed him into the house. She asked Homer if he would like her to fix him something to eat before she left. He told her that there was still a little left-over chicken in the refrigerator, and he would look to see what else was available. He said that he was not used to having to think about meal prep and this was not going to be easy. They rounded up enough vegetables to go with the chicken that it was a surprisingly good meal.

Alice wanted to break the ice and asked, "Homer would you like me to come out here and help you with meals and the house for a while. We could do it together and you would have more time to take care of your animals. You got those fifty new chicks today and I know that you need to have eight rabbits for the restaurant on Saturday. You are not used to doing it alone and I would like to help if you will let me."

Homer somberly replied, "I know that I told you how much I like your company and wanted to spend more time with you, but this is not what I expected. I know that my uncle and aunt have said that I could eat there and maybe we could be together for a couple of days and I could eat there a couple of days. I do not want to make your parents question what we are doing out here alone during this time. You mean a lot to me, and I do not want to be a bother or get you in trouble. I want to thank you for going with me tonight and staying with me while we were there. I know my momma will like you when she wakes up and meets you."

They finished their meal and Alice said she would stop by during her lunch break, and they could decide about tomorrow night and the cooking. It was Homer tonight who took her in his arms and held her close and kissed her on the cheek before she left. The house seemed overly quiet as Homer went up to his room for the night. He did what he had said earlier and asked Jesus to heal his momma, so she could come home and meet Alice.

Homer, Jake, and Alice were speaking together during lunch in the office of the garage. Flora was planning for Homer to have his meal with them this evening, so Alice said that she would bring a meal to the farm the next day and go with them to the hospital again. The conversation was not very cheerful, but Homer did walk Alice to her car and thank her before she left.

They were in the room with Sis that night and she was moaning when spoken to and could move her right leg and as well as her fingers a little. They were all very encouraged by that progress as they told her goodnight and left her in the room one more time.

Chapter Eleven

Homer and Alice were on their way to deliver the rabbit meat to the restaurant on Saturday as planned. They were going to go to the hospital as soon as they were done. Homer collected his money from the owner and was about to leave when the owner asked him if he could bring ten rabbits the following week. Homer took a minute to think about how many rabbits he had in the litter back home and said it would be no problem. He was going to have to take the time to build some more brooding pens soon.

Two nights ago, Sis had opened her eyes as they spoke to her, and she tried to hold Homer's hand with her right hand. She had done similarly last night but they were hoping that she would progress quickly. The nurses had said that they were going to try to get her into a chair this afternoon and Homer was anxious to see how she was doing as they drove there. Alice had been with him every chance that she could and had brought one meal from her mother and was planning on baking a chicken when they got back home today. The two of them were finding it quite easy to be together even with the stress on Homer with his momma.

They arrived at the hospital, and they walked in holding hands as they had become accustomed to doing. Homer peeked into his mother's room from behind the door and saw her sitting in a chair with some straps around her to help her stay in the chair. The straps went across her flaccid left arm and under her right, so she could move it around. It became obvious as she was sitting up that the left side of her face drooped, and her left shoulder was hanging lower than the right. Homer took the first step into the room and said, "Would you look at my momma sitting there pretty as a lilac blossom in the springtime."

Sis looked in his direction at the sound of his voice. She tried to raise her arm but only her hand up to her wrist moved. Homer took it gently into his hand and started to speak to her some more. He said, "Alice came with me again today momma. She has been helping me with the housework and Aunt Flora has helped me some too. We have kept it so that it will not be too big a mess when you come home in a little while. I must admit that I may have lost some of the plants you had started for the garden because I forgot to water them for a few days. I will start you some more when you get ready to come home."

Sis was sitting there doing a little fidgeting as she listened, and she had a tear coming down the right side of her face. She let out a moan, but you could not tell if it was a word or pain that made her do it. She finally closed her eyes and let her hand go limp at her side. Homer gently picked it back up and held it in his hand again. She opened her eyes again and there was another tear running down her cheek. The nurses came by her room and were going to put her back into her bed, but they said they would leave her up for a little while with Homer.

Homer continued to speak to her as she sat there and her

trying to communicate back became less and less as he spoke. Alice told Homer that she was obviously tired and that they should go so they could put her back into her bed and let her rest. Homer was reluctant at first, but he considered his momma's eyes and there was no sparkle there at all. He finally agreed, and they told the nurse that they were leaving so she could go back to bed.

As they were driving back to the farm, Alice tried to get Homer to think about something different than his momma. She asked, "How would you like me to fix your chicken for supper today. Do you like it spicy or with just some poultry seasoning? I could fix you some of that long grain brown rice if you would like and I could bake a casserole with the left over. I found a jar of pickled beets that I could heat to go with it."

Homer thought for a minute and said, "We can't have it too spicy if we are going to make a casserole tomorrow. I need to do some work with the animals today before it gets too late."

Alice smiled and said, "Could I go and see the new chicks? I have never seen them growing before. I really have never seen much of the farm in daylight as far as that goes. I would like to know what makes you happy."

Homer dryly replied, "I have the animals so there can be meat on the table and not for fun. There were many years that if I did not have any luck snaring rabbits or catching fish there was no meat for our meals. Now I have found a way to sell the eggs at the store and rabbit meat at the restaurants, so it does not take any of my pay from the garage to feed them as well as having meat for us and my uncle. I still hunt occasionally but it is easier to control the food on the table if you can go out to a coop to get it. I bought the freezer earlier this winter so that I could slaughter more than one animal as we needed it. I have found a fur trader that will pay me almost a dollar per skin for my rabbit pelts if I skin them correctly. That is more than it costs to feed it to the time of slaughter so the money for the meat is profit. My uncle has been teaching me about making a profit because he wants to sell me the servíce station soon."

Alice responded as they drove, "It sounds like a wonderful plan, and I would like to learn how I could help you with them. I do not know if I want to kill them, but I could help you get them ready to go to the restaurant and things like that if you want me to. If you were not so concerned for your momma, would you still be spending time with me because you wanted to? I do not mean to be crude with my questions, but this certainly must be an incredibly stressful time for you, and I want you to know that I am not doing this because of my pity for you. I am doing it because I want to be with you and share this time with you."

Homer's voice was a little snappy, "I have told you before that I do not know how to be around people very well. I am glad that you are here with me, but I do not know if it is the way for people who really care for each other to act or just to be neighborly.

I know what part of me wants it to be, but I do not want to hurt you with the way I may be acting. The only person who has ever really helped me is my Uncle Jake, but I do not think of you like I think of my uncle. I have been alone so much of my life that the loneliness had become easy to bear. If I never saw you again, I would just go back to being alone, but I do not want to do that. I want to be with you and that is how I feel. If that is love, then I have grown to love you."

Alice smiled as she faced him and said, "I knew that I loved you from the first time we had that picnic at the lake. You are the kindest, gentlest man, I have ever met. You are always considerate of my feelings, and I have never found you offensive to anyone and especially to me."

They were just getting to the farm and before they got out of the car, they kissed each other on the lips. Homer went to the other side of the car and held the door for her. The shadows were getting longer so they went to see the new chicks before going to the house. They all scampered around as Homer tried to let Alice hold one in her hand. She nestled it against her cheek and spoke to it as if she expected it to understand. Homer just smiled at her as she put it back down on the ground. Homer saw that his uncle had already changed the water today, so they went into the house.

Homer took the chicken out of the refrigerator and told Alice that she would have to look for whatever she needed because he did not know where his momma kept anything. He told her that he had to go and have a doe rabbit bred and he would be back shortly. Homer did a quick check to make sure that he would have the ten rabbits for the restaurant the following Saturday. Five of them had to grow quickly to get near the two pounds that the restaurant wanted them to weigh but he could wait to slaughter them until Friday if he had to. He was looking at where he could place the other pens that he had to build when his uncle came walking over. He wanted to get a couple of the chickens that were in the freezer to put in their refrigerator for them. Homer went to the house with him, so he could check on how Alice was doing with their meal. Homer told his uncle how they had his momma up in a chair and how frustrated she had become when she could not speak. Jake told him that they would teach her how to answer questions if she was unable to speak. He said that she would probably get strong enough to write some words or point to some cards with pictures to indicate what she wanted like food or water. Homer finally said what was on his mind about his fear of her not coming home. His uncle said that it was too early to think about that and to just take one day at a time. His uncle also reminded him that he wanted to go back to showing Homer how to run the garage and do the bookkeeping. Homer said they could start again this week if nothing else came up.

Alice and Homer shared their meal once it got cooked. It was a little later than usual with Alice having to look for everything that she needed. When they were done, Alice deboned the rest of the chicken and washed the casserole dish that she had used to cook the chicken in. She put the rice and the chicken into the dish and refrigerated it all. She told Homer that it would only take thirty minutes to bake it once she added the last of the ingredients to the dish. They spent a short time together after the meal and then Alice went home for the night.

Homer and his uncle were doing the paperwork for the day before during their lunch time. They were surprised by a man in a suit walking into the garage. His uncle said hello to the man and asked him if he could help him. The man introduced himself and told them that he had come from their bank as Jake had requested. Jake told the man that he was surprised by his coming to the building and had expected to go to the bank to see him. The man said that they always inspected a building that they were proposing to give a loan for prior to any negotiations. Jake said that they would be glad to show him the building and some of the paperwork that they needed in their consideration of the loan. Homer stood there listening and almost fell over when the man asked him if he was going to be the buyer. Jake quickly spoke up and introduced Homer and told him yes that he was the buyer. He told the man that they were just going over the prior day's income and he could look at that if he wanted to. The man did look at it and asked how near to average the income was. Jake told him that it was a little lower than average, but their work was coming in very consistently. Jake explained that they only paid for the gasoline that they sold during the week. A company rep would come by and read the meters at the gas pumps, and they would write him a check for what they had sold. The banker asked him if they took credit cards yet and said they could get the service from the bank for a minimal fee. Jake told him that they would be extremely interested in finding out how that worked. They showed the man around and gave him a basic list of their inventory. The banker told them that no part of the loan could pay for the inventory that was involved in the sale. They all ended up at the office again and the banker told them, "You need to get an official sales contract written up between the two of you and how it does not include the inventory in the amount requested in the loan. If you are gifting him a portion of the value of the business, it must be shown in the sales contract as well. Please drop that off at the bank at your earliest convenience and we will set up a new meeting after that. Good day gentlemen."

Homer stood next to his uncle after the man left and said, "I wasn't aware that you had spoken to a banker about selling me the business. Do you think that I am ready for this?"

Jake said, "I totally believe in you and this service station. You can increase business if you get involved with taking credit cards. They have been around for a few years and more people are starting to use them. The money goes into your account the next day and it is as good as cash if the card were approved. You could also get credit cards from the company that sells us gasoline and you give him the credit card receipts when the rep comes around and only the balance would come out of your checking account. We have been talking about doing this for a while and with Sis having her stroke, I want to do it right away. I do not say that to be mean or to seem angry. I just want to do some things with Flora before I go to my grave. As far as giving you some of the value as a gift, you can consider it my wedding present to you and Alice. You didn't think I was observing you without some inclination of what is going on did you?"

Homer just grinned at the comment. He said, "I believe I love her, but I do not have much experience being around other people, so I am nervous about the whole thing. I think I will go back to work for a while and think about some of this."

Chapter Twelve

Homer was outside taking care of the animals and Alice was inside making the casserole later that night. Homer noticed that another of his does had a litter during the last twenty-four hours since he had been out there. He knew in his mind that it would be better if he could find a new line of rabbits to add to his breeder does. He was not sure where to look but maybe Alice could give him some ideas. When he got into the house, he asked her how to find a new line of rabbits somewhere.

"I have never looked but I would start in the back of magazines in the personal ads of things for sale," Alice answered. "I will look during some of my free time when I am at the library and copy down any information you might be able to use. You could even put an ad of your own in the local paper and tell people how to find you. I will have the dinner ready in about fifteen minutes. How did it go at work today?"

Homer fudged a little before he said, "I was going to speak to you about it later, but we can speak about it now and see what you think. My uncle and I were eating lunch in the office and going over yesterday's books when a banker stopped by to see the building. My uncle has stepped up when he wants to sell me the garage because of momma's being sick. In his own words, he wants to do things with Aunt Flora before they are too old to enjoy them. He said that he was sure I was ready and then we spoke about accepting credit cards to increase our business. He said a couple of other things, but I do not want to tell you about them now."

"That is okay, you do not have to tell me anything you do not want to," Alice said. "Were you happy to hear the news?"

Homer enthusiastically said, "I was surprised at the timing, but we have had this planned for quite a while. He will still be around most of the time for a while, so I can ask him things when necessary. I still have trouble with keeping an inventory that meets our needs but does not make us short of cash each week. I have heard that you can create a soft partnership with some of the parts dealers in town and work from their inventory and they give you extra services like free delivery as quick as they can during the day. It would be like the gasoline we pump in that what we get is what we pay for at the end of the week. Each week I would pay for the parts that we had put in the cars and got paid for. It would minimize our inventory to a minimum and could really increase our business at the same time."

Alice thoughtfully said, "I don't know how anyone ever called you stupid because you surely have a talent at running this business. I believe in you, and I hope that you can get the loan right away. I think our dinner should be ready by now. I will check the oven and you can get cleaned up for dinner. I gave this a special touch and I hope you like it."

They sat at the table and started to eat the casserole and

Alice watched Homer's eyes smile at the new taste. He said, "This is fantastic, but I am not sure what you added to get it to taste fruity and sweet like this."

Alice admitted, "I added a cup of cooking wine to the finished casserole and let it bake an extra five minutes to evaporate the alcohol. All you have left in the dish is the wine without the alcohol and it gives it that fruity taste. I hope you like it as much as you say you do. It is a trick that my mother taught me as we were cooking together. That reminds me that my mother would like to have you come over for dinner this weekend. I thought that we could do it after you delivered the rabbit meat to the restaurant and stopped at the hospital to see your momma."

"I guess I want to meet them, but you may be embarrassed at how I might act," Homer said sheepishly. "The only time that I have not eaten at home was when I was working for some of the farmers near where I live. I don't even know what your father does for work or what your mother is like."

Alice declared, "That is the whole purpose of having you come to the house for a meal. They want to meet you. They have been concerned about how your mother has been doing and I keep them informed with what I know. You will meet my brother and younger sister if it is on a weekend. My brother stays at the college during the week where he teaches English Composition. My sister is a receptionist for a company in town that sells insurance. You will not have to act any differently with them than you do with me as far as being with them. My daddy does the bookkeeping for businesses in the area that have large payrolls and need to plan how to spend their money during the business year. My mom stays at home and baby sits for some mothers who need to work in the area. We are almost normal people that you could meet anywhere on a given day."

Homer questioned, "What is not normal about you and your family that I should know about? I don't want to insult anyone by mistake."

Alice just laughed at his comment and then said, "I am not normal because I love you. The part about my family was just a joke. If we were all normal in this world, we would all be alike and each of us in the world was created to be who we are and different from each other. That is all that I meant about not being normal."

Homer gave it some thought and said, "I get it. There is no reason to fear meeting them because I have not met them before. I would be glad to go to your parents' house after we get done at the hospital. We may have to stop at a store somewhere this weekend and get some groceries for my house. I will have to buy bread, so I do not have to make biscuits and stuff like that with the little time that I can spend at home. I will make a list with you after supper, and I will get what you want to have here."

"Are you secretly trying to find out if I know how to keep a house and not being direct about it," Alice quizzed. "Your momma and I are not the same in the way we would do the same things in a house. Part of being married to a person is learning how to please them in ways only you know how. She could teach me where the seasoning is kept in her kitchen but only you can tell me if I do it the way you like it. For example, you can consider the wine that I put in the casserole tonight. Your momma may never have tried that in a recipe, but I knew how to do it and you enjoyed it."

Homer said defensively, "I know that you are not my momma and that is why I asked if you wanted to make part of the list for the kitchen. I miss my momma, but I do not want to make you be like her. I want to know what it would be like to be with you and make you happy. You see, I don't know how to be around people." He turned and walked out of the room.

Alice let him walk out of the room without saying anything to him as he went. She looked around the cabinets in the kitchen for items that she might want to find to bake or cook with. She put a few items on the list that she could not find including flour and corn meal. She only wrote out canned fruit not knowing what ones Homer liked. She found some cooking lard and a can of shortening both in the cabinets. She found a jar of yeast in the refrigerator as well as some pickles. She had a finished list when Homer came back into the room, and she handed it to him. She said, "I would like some of these items if you would and you might add some ham or beef to the list if you want me to fix them."

Homer looked at the list quietly and then went to a door leading to a shed attached to the house. He beckoned Alice to him and showed her a large metal box and said, "The extra flour and sugar are in there so varmints can't get to them. We also have some beef in the freezer from a heifer that we slaughtered last fall. We are going to do at least one more very soon and we will have half the meat from it and my uncle will have the rest. If you would like some ham, I like it very much also. Is this a time when I should say that I am sorry for what I said?"

Alice smiled at him again and said, "I not only think you should apologize but I think you should kiss me and make it better."

Homer was more than willing to comply with her request.

Homer and Alice were on their way to deliver the rabbits to the restaurant on Saturday. Alice asked, "Will you tell me how your meeting went with the bank yesterday?"

Homer answered, "I almost went to see you last night to tell you all about it, but I knew we would be together today, so I waited. The loan for the sale has already been approved and we only need to get some legal documents ready for the bank and Uncle Jake will get his money and I will be a business owner. It went through so quickly because of how little Uncle Jake asked me for the business. Remember the first day we were speaking about this, and I told you I did not want to tell you everything we had discussed about the loan?"

"I remember I told you to tell me what you wanted me to know, and I have not asked you about it since," Alice responded.

Homer started again, "The loan went through because Uncle Jake gifted me one third of the total value of the business. When I asked him about it, he said for me to consider it a wedding present to us. I did not want to mention it in any way until I was certain of what I wanted and how things were looking for in the future. I also have something in my shirt pocket that I want to give you before we go to your parents later."

Homer pulled out an engagement ring from his shirt pocket and held it out in his hand. He said, "Alice, will you marry me?" He had to stop the car on the side of the road, so they would not go into the ditch as Alice grabbed him around the neck and gave him a kiss with her answer. He continued, "I know that I am supposed to ask your father for his permission to marry you and I will do that tonight while we are there. I also intend to tell my momma about it while we are at the hospital. Now if you will stop kissing me long enough that we can get my work done, I will drive to the restaurant."

Alice was like a young girl as she wiggled and squirmed in the seat as she looked at the engagement ring on her finger from different angles. She said, "I have never seen anything so lovely in my life. I will make you proud for having married me. I may have to take it off long enough for you to ask my daddy and then put it back on. Will you hurry up and get to the restaurant; I want to kiss you again."

Homer delivered the rabbit meat finally and told the owner that he would only have eight rabbits ready for the following week. Homer told him how he had found some more does this week and they were to be delivered to the farm on Sunday. The owner was okay with that and commented to Homer on how well his patrons liked the flavor of his rabbits.

Alice and Homer went to the hospital next. His momma was up in a chair as was customary for the afternoons there. She was now able to take Homer by the hand when he came over, but she could not say a word. They were helping her learn to write on a tablet that they would hold near her hand. Alice went over to her and held out her hand with the engagement ring on her finger. Sis could touch the ring and nodded her head ever so slightly to Alice. She patted Alice's hand but there formed a tear in her eye that happened when she really wanted to speak. They handed her a pencil and held the pad for her as she tried to form some letters. The first word turned out to be good and the second word became happy. They spent some more time with her until it became obvious that she was very tired.

Homer and Alice pulled up in front of her parents' house and Alice had Homer put the ring back in his pocket for a few minutes. It was as Alice had told him to expect with her entire family in the house when they got there. The house was nice and tidy with the smell of the meal filling the room. It was her mother that Homer met first. She said, "Hello Homer. I am Evelyn Moodie. Welcome to our home."

Homer responded, "Thank you for inviting me Mrs. Moodie." He was then brought to the living room where her father was sitting. Homer could instantly see by the extra pounds on Mr. Moodie that he was not given to physical activities.

Her father stood up and held out his hand to Homer and said, "Hello Homer, I am Harold Moodie. I am sorry to hear how sick your momma has been."

Homer said, "Thank you Mr. Moodie. I don't know what I would have done for the last few weeks without Alice at my side."

Her brother was next, and he said, "Hello Homer. I am her brother James. I am only here on weekends, but it is nice to meet you."

Homer shook his hand and said, "Thank you James. Alice said you stay at the college where you teach during the week during the school year."

He was already being introduced to a bouncy young lady in slacks and a wind breaker that could easily be recognized as Alice's sister. She said, "Hello Homer. I am Susan and I am dressed like this because a group of us are going for a run after we have our meal. We run a few miles together for safety and challenge."

Homer smiled as he said, "It is very nice to meet you Susan, but I will not be running those miles with you tonight." Most of them laughed at his comment. Homer was invited to have a seat near Mr. Moodie and the women went to get the meal onto the table. Homer said, "I was told by Alice that you do bookkeeping for companies in the area. I have been learning how to care for the books at the service station before I buy it. My uncle is selling it to me right now, so he and my aunt can do some traveling before they get too old to enjoy it. He was bothered by what happened to his sister and he has decided that it is a good time to do it."

James could see that they were going to talk shop, so he excused himself and left the room. Homer started again, "I am glad that James has left the room because I have a question for you. I have only known your daughter for a couple of months, but we fell in love together in that time. It is my intention to ask you to allow me to marry your daughter."

It was obvious by the way that Mr. Moodie gasped that he was not expecting that kind of a question on the first day they met. He said, "Homer, I just met you about ten minutes ago and I don't know anything about you except what Alice has told us and that is not much. You just mentioned that you are buying the service station from your uncle where you have been working. I know that you live in a house on your uncle's farm, and it was with your momma until she got sick recently. Am I right so far?"

Homer was starting to feel queasy because he did not get

the immediate yes that he was expecting but he was not going to quit that easily. He said, "You are right to that point. The house does belong to my uncle, but I will be inheriting the entire farm when they are gone. It was my grandfather's, and they want it to stay in the family. The service station was started by my grandfather as well and that is why they are selling it to me. On the farm we raise chickens, cows, and rabbits for meat for ourselves as well as selling some to restaurants. I like all the work that I do, and I make a good living doing it and could provide a good home for us."

Mr. Moodie surprised him again and said that he was going to ask his wife and Alice to come into the room for a couple of minutes. Susan was left in charge of watching the pots on the stove as the women came back to the living room. Mr. Moodie looked at his wife and said, "We are just meeting Homer for the first time, and he has asked me for permission to marry Alice. We have been discussing what kind of life they would have as far as work or money but there is so much more to a marriage."

Alice looked like she was going to cry but Homer held his ground and kept his eyes on Mr. Moodie. Mrs. Moodie said, "I am not surprised by the question because mother and daughter speak more openly than you men. I know that they love each other but they have not known each other for long at all. When do they want to do this?"

Homer answered her that they certainly had not set a date

without their consent but that he would like to do it in a couple of months or less. The parents looked at Alice as she walked over to Homer and put her hand in his. It was silent for a couple of minutes as Mr. Moodie rubbed his chin deep in thought. He finally said, "Alice do you wish to marry this man whom you have known for such a short time?"

Alice was quick to answer, "Yes daddy. I do want to marry this man. I have never met a man like him. He is the most honest and genuine man that has no malice in him. He has a lot of reasons to be angry with the world, but he chooses to just live the best he can. He is willing to change what he can, and he is willing to accept the things he cannot change. I gave him his first taste of wine the other day when I cooked with it, and I know that he loves me."

Mr. Moodie said, "I hope I don't come to regret this, but I give you permission to marry our daughter."

Alice quickly took Homer in her arms and kissed him. He took the ring back out of his pocket and asked Alice from one knee if she would marry him. She said yes again and then the congratulations started as she placed the ring on her finger.

It took several minutes for the commotion to settle down after that. Her sister gave her a big hug as well as her brother. They both made fun of her being the first to get married in the family, but it was all in jest. They finally sat at the table and enjoyed a wonderful beef roast with all the fixings. Mrs. Moodie did ask

Homer if he attended any church, and he told her about going to Pastor Murray's church. She asked him if Alice's church would be okay for the wedding and Homer said he would do anything to make her happy.

Chapter Thirteen

Homer was already at work on Monday when his uncle came to work. He asked Homer how Saturday had gone, and he was all smiles. His uncle said he wanted to hear all about it at lunch. Homer did not even give him a hint as to how well it had gone. He had not told his uncle about having bought an engagement ring and his plan to propose marriage to Alice.

The two men were talking over lunch and his uncle said he looked like the cat that had swallowed the canary and he better spit it out before it choked him. Homer said, "We had an exceptionally good roast beef dinner with her parents on Saturday night. I got to meet the entire family when we first got there. I was just speaking to her father when her brother left the room, and I had a chance to ask him if I could marry his daughter."

His uncle let out a "What did you ask him?"

Homer said, "I asked him if I could marry his daughter. He did not give me a quick yes or no, so we spoke for a while longer. He knew that I was buying the garage from you, but he wanted to know where we might live and stuff like that. Then he got Mrs. Moodie and Alice, and both came to the living room with us. Her mother and Alice had already been talking about our being in love, so it was not as big a surprise for her. He asked Alice if she wanted to marry me, and she told him yes and why. He then committed to allowing us to marry. I took the ring out of my pocket and proposed to her in front of her entire family."

His uncle said, "Congratulations! I did not know when you were going to propose to Alice but the first time that you meet her parents is hurrying things. I am surprised he did not throw you out of his house. I'm only kidding," his uncle added as he saw the look come over Homer's face.

"We got to tell my momma when we were at the hospital," Homer said. "She gets so mad when she cannot speak. Then she gets tired, and we must leave. She did write on the paper we held for her. I'm never going to be able to bring her home, am I?"

His uncle said, "They have called me in private from the hospital and asked me where I wanted her to live out the rest of her life. I have known that from the very first day, but I did not want to discourage you until you had time to think about it and see how she is going to be. She is never coming home with us again."

Homer did not respond but got up and went back to work. He would not say another word that day until he was with Alice later at the farm. They had gone to the farm and Alice was in the kitchen and Homer was in the coops. He had gotten six more does and their pens yesterday from someone in the next county. The pens were made of metal and were off the ground about three feet. The seller told him that three of the does were bred and he might be able to use a buck from the offspring to change his breeding line a little. He now had enough rabbits to supply another restaurant as well as the one he was dealing with now. They were at the table ready to eat when Alice asked him what was going on that was making him so quiet. She asked him if he was upset with things from the weekend and finally, he spoke.

Homer tearfully said, "I am never going to be able to bring my momma home again. The doctor has been speaking to my uncle and asking him where we would like her to live. I know I cannot change what has happened and I know that I cannot take care of her. I just had to let go of that last ray of hope that I had been holding on to for so long. If you tell me what you would like to change in the house, I will start to make it so that you like the way it is."

Alice carefully said, "We don't have to change anything today, Homer. I thank you for thinking of me in those regards. I may try to put the kitchen cabinets a little more to the way that I am used to, but the rest of the house can wait. Have you spoken to Pastor Murray since your momma got sick? You might do well with going over and speaking to him. I don't have to go unless you want me to."

The following Tuesday night, the two of them were on their way to see Pastor Mike Murray at the church. There was a car in the parking lot and there was a light on in the hallway to the chapel. Pastor Mike heard them enter and came to greet them from a side room. He invited them to come in, so they would be more comfortable in nice chairs. Pastor Mike said, "I still thank Jesus that he sent someone along who could fix my car the day that you helped me. I have heard that your momma is not doing well now, and I suppose that is why you came to speak to me. I believe that the other reason is sitting in the other chair with a smile on her face."

Homer could feel his face blush as he looked at Pastor Mike and said, "Pastor Mike, I would like you to meet Alice Moodie, my fiancée."

They took time to greet each other, and Homer started again, "I have learned over the years that there are some things in life that you cannot change but there are some things that you would like to be different. It is true that my momma had a very severe stroke and can no longer speak or move her left side. I will never be able to bring her back home and I wish I could change that. I go and see her with Alice, and we can tell that she hears us but cannot answer with her voice. She can write a few words on paper before she gets all tired out and I wish I could change that. I have prayed to Jesus that he would make my momma better, but I don't think even he can do that for me now."

Pastor Mike interjected, "What you mean is that Jesus could heal her with a miracle, but you are not sure that he is going to do that. I cannot tell you that He is going to, but he certainly could if He decided to. This is as hard for you as if she had died that day with your emotions, but it is made more difficult for you because you cannot change something you want very badly, and you don't have the comfort of knowing that she could be with Jesus instead of suffering the way she is. We have the assurance as believers of knowing that we will be with Jesus and His Father one day at the time of our death. That day will end all our earthly suffering and we will have a new body with Jesus in heaven. I don't have a solid answer as to why some people are asked to suffer so on this earth, but we have a hope of things yet to come."

Homer said with tears in his eyes, "I have felt bad that I have wished that my momma had gone to be with Jesus that day. Instead, I get to watch her suffer and I cannot even bring her home. I do not know if I could stand it if Alice had not been there to help me keep my feelings under control. She is a wonderful woman, and I can hardly wait to make her my wife."

Pastor Mike said, "Are you ready for marriage Homer? Have the two of you been speaking about things that are going to come along in life and agree on how you will take care of them? Have you spoken of having children and if so, how many do you both want to have? Have you spoken about working outside of the home both now and after the children come? Have you decided where you are going to live? I do not get to see you very often, Homer, and I do not know Alice at all. I make sure that the people that I marry have discussed these things before they get to the altar and commit to a lifetime together. How are things going to be between the two of you when you both have grey hair, and you can no longer work? The things you see and feel today will change with time if it is not real love for one another that brings you to that altar. I know that you did not come here to ask me to marry you so let us talk about your momma some more."

Homer softly said, "She will be going to a care home for people who cannot take care of themselves. I am sure she would like to see you, but she will not be able to speak with you. Thank you for seeing me today and we will be going along now."

Homer stood and started for the door with Alice close behind him. Pastor Mike said, "Homer, I would like to have you come back here and sit down and speak to me for a few minutes more if you would. You have taken offense with the things I have said, and I want to speak to you for just a few more minutes."

Homer slowly stopped his walk and turned around and followed the hand commands to come back into the room. Homer said, "You are right, and you do not know me well and this is the first time you have met Alice. What makes you think that you can tell us what to do if you do not know us?"

Pastor Mike said, "You are right. I should have asked you more questions before giving you directions. Tell me some things that I might want to know about the two of you and how you met."

Homer added, "Alice used to come into the service station to buy gas and I finally got the nerve to ask her out. I really do not know how to act outside of our home with people because it has only been momma and me. I was never around girls because I never went to school. We went to the lake one day for a picnic and I told Alice just those things and she has never made fun of me when I had to ask if I was doing things right. I never knew what real love was and we had to discuss my feelings and emotions because of what I had never seen or been around. I had all the right feelings, but I did not know what they were. My uncle has taught me some of the general things and Alice has forgiven me for things I did not know. I do know that I love her, and I want to be around her and make her happy. I am buying the service station from my uncle, and we will be living on the farm where I was with my momma. The entire farm will be mine when my aunt and uncle pass away. I also have chickens, cows, and rabbits that we raise on the farm. I sell eggs and rabbit meat enough to make a profit from that also. I will let Alice tell you something about herself now."

Alice then responded, "I am so proud of Homer, and I love him very much. I had to go by the station several times before he finally asked me out. I thought that I might have to ask him. I live at home with my parents, and I work at the library in town. What Homer does not know is what makes him such a wonderful man. He wants his life to be better than it was, but he will not hurt anyone to have it that way. The fact that he asks me so often if he has hurt me or done something wrong proves to me how much he cares, and we are learning together. He has a plan for his life, but it is well grounded and not as if he is chasing something he cannot have. I thought that I might lose him to his own emotions when his momma had a stroke but his resolve to accept the things, he cannot change triumphed over the pain he was suffering. He is a good mechanic and loves what he does, and I love him."

Pastor Mike said, "It sounds as if you two are going at this with your eyes wide open and knowing what you want. I do suggest you give some of my suggestions and have some discussion before they sneak up on you and you are not ready. Most people have no idea how much a baby will change their lives when it is born. Homer, I did not mean to offend you by telling you what I ask anyone who is thinking of getting married and I wish you both the best that Jesus can give you."

The three of them said their goodbyes and they went their separate ways.

Homer was trying to figure out a way to give his rabbits shade as the summer heat approached them. He wanted to stop some of the sun, but he also had to allow the breeze to reach them. He decided that he might have to build a shed just to put all the rabbits in or at least a roof with two sides. There was a builder in town that used their services and Homer decided to ask him for ideas the next time he saw him.

Homer was at the service station the next morning and his uncle was later than normal. When he arrived, he called Homer to the office. He said, "I have decided to take the day off. Your aunt is in the car waiting for me and we are going to go to town today. I am no longer going to run this station, but you are. I will be around here or at the farm for a while, but you are to take the work, do the estimates, and get the work done. I will oversee the books as you want me to, but I think you should get Alice to learn how to check your work. Her father is an accountant, and I am sure that she has learned some of his work processes over the years. You need to get to the bank as soon as possible and find out about the credit cards and you can speak to the gas rep again this week. I told him to bring you all the papers you would need this week when he comes. I will take no more paychecks and you will have to learn how to figure Ron's hours each week. He is always owed one week's pay, so you will have a week to figure it out and have it ready for him on his payday. He is a good man and can be trusted. I have asked him, and he wants to stay and work for you. You already know how much money is in the checking account and I am adding that to the sale. It is all yours to start this with. Do you have any questions?"

Homer said, "I know where you live so I can ask you later if I have a need. I was wondering if you were going to go and see momma today."

Jake hesitated but said, "I wish you hadn't asked but I will not lie to you. The doctor wants us to find a place for her to go to, so they can have the hospital bed for other people. I will let you know what we find today and what there is for a plan. We are going to speak to the people at Mavis House before we leave town and ask them if she could live there for a while. I will let you know before we do anything that would make it difficult to see her."

His uncle stood up and left the station at that time and Homer had to go out and pump some gas for a customer. He was on his own now. Alice came by during her lunch and Homer told her about his uncle having left the station for him to run from now on. Alice said something that caught Homer off guard when she stated, "I don't know how we will be able to go away for a honeymoon now your uncle has left."

Homer made a point of getting an appointment to find out how to take credit cards when he went to make the deposit in the afternoon. They gave him an information sheet to look at before the set time to meet. He took it back with him to the station and put it with the papers he would be taking home from now on. He found himself thinking that life was moving a lot faster than it had for the first twenty years of his life.

Homer was working on a car in the bay when he had to go out and pump some gas for a customer. He did not recognize the car, but he certainly recognized Harold Moodie sitting in the driver's seat. They greeted each other and then Homer filled his car with gasoline. He accepted the payment from Mr. Moodie and thanked him for the business. Then Mr. Moodie asked him if he was going to need someone to help him with the bookkeeping for the station. Homer told him they could speak about it later when he was not so busy, and they agreed to do that. Homer turned and walked away from his car with one of those queasy feelings in the pit of his stomach.

Alice came to the farm to fix dinner as she was becoming accustomed to doing. Homer did his chores quietly and they joined each other at the dinner table as usual. Homer said, "I saw your father today at the station when he came and bought gasoline for his car. Then he came right out and asked me if I would hire him to keep my books for the station."

Alice let out a gasp and said, "I'm so sorry Homer. I do not know why he does things like that. I can have a talk with him, and he will not get mad at me when I tell him no and why. I am not going to give him the chance to know how your business in doing by being sneaky in that manner. He makes me so angry sometimes."

Homer questioningly said, "I hope I can keep up with taking on credit cards and doing the estimates and working. Life was really a lot simpler a short time ago. I got a pamphlet from the bank today that we should read about taking credit cards. I guess from what I can see that you imprint the card on this form, and you must write in what you sold on it. You total it up and you have them sign it. They get a soft copy, and you get a firmer copy. You add them into your deposit like you do a check and the money goes onto your account. It says we are responsible for having all the numbers visible and that the dates on the cards are valid. If they are not, they will take the money back out of your account and give you the bad cards back, so you can try and get your money some other way. People can use it to get their cars fixed if they do not go over a certain limit. I know that the banks are trying to make it safer for people to travel and not have as much cash on them, but it seems to me that we should try to get cash as often as we can."

Alice said, "The other side of that coin is the fact that we would have less cash available for someone to steal if we were ever robbed. I will learn to help you with some of the paperwork as it comes along. One of the things that I have heard my father suggest to people repeatedly is to not have the amount of your checking account balance where anyone can find it. He says that you should have a ledger with your deposits and balance away from the checkbook, so no one knows how well your station is doing. That has always sounded like good advice to me. There is one thing that I want to speak to you about tonight if possible. I would like us to pick a date that we want to get married on."

Homer said, "I am going to let you be happy with this decision and I do not care if it is soon. If we had decided to be together, and I believe that we have, I would like to do it soon. I have a small family to invite and no friends to speak to so that does not pose a problem. What did you have in mind for us?"

Alice said, "My mother wants to invite several people from around town that we do business with and some of my family. We counted nearly fifty people on her list, but I have never seen everyone come that is invited to a wedding. I was looking at a calendar today and wondered if the fifteenth of next month would be okay with you. That gives us five weeks to get ready and I have already checked with our pastor and that date is still open for him. He also wanted to meet with us some night next week if we could."

Chapter Fourteen

Homer was meeting with the gas representative on Friday when he came for his weekly meeting. Homer was discussing with him how he was now operating the garage and how he wanted to take credit cards from his customers. The rep said, "Congratulations on your new business. Our company has made it quite simple for you to take credit cards. You will use the same imprinter that the bank will supply you with, but you will use our forms. They will be easy to separate from the bank ones as you prepare your deposits. You will have some slips to list them on just like the bank and you will give them to me when I come on Fridays. We will take the entire amount that you owe for the week for gas, and we will subtract the amount of the credit card slips to find the amount that you will write the check for. It might be the right time to discuss with you a new program that our company is offering for someone just like you. The world is changing around us, and we need to change to keep up. If you sign a contract with our company for the exclusive sale of whatever products we offer at your station, we will come in and install new gas tanks, at least two new gas pumps, and install a canopy with our company logo so people do not have to stand in the rain to get their gas pumped. It is also possible to improve the front of your station if we install our logos. This would be done for no charge to you. We would have an engineer come and create a plan for your entire lot and for the flow of traffic. They would get with your town and make sure that we would not get in the way of anything they have planned for the area. You will have the opportunity to make some minor adjustments to the plan if it needs to be done but we would do and pay for the work."

Homer exclaimed, "Wow! That sounds like a great deal. I only sell your products now, but you would want a contract from me that I would sell your products."

The rep explained, "It is the way that the company can be sure that the work that they are offering to do has a return for them. If you allowed us to do the work for you and we had no contract, another company could come in and offer to sell you gas for less money. We are not saying that you would, but it is a good faith gesture for our mutual benefit."

Homer asked, "What does mutual mean?"

The rep explained again, "Mutual means that it benefits both parties. You would have modern new pumps and a new store front, and we would have a place that sold only our products. It would be mutually beneficial. Think about it this week and when I come back next week, I will have the credit card slips and agreement to use them with me if you choose to do credit cards. Again, I say congratulations to you. If you still see your uncle, ask him for his opinion about it this week."

Homer followed the rep out to the front of the building, and they discussed some options as he got into his car. The building had not had any work done on it in over twenty years, so a new front could help his business.

Homer also had a talk with the people at the parts store about the soft contracts and what it could mean to him. They told him that it was little more than an agreement of loyalty with the use of credit for a week at a time. They said they offered it because they saved time over getting paid for every little transaction and the operator could be in and out faster. He would sign a slip with the price that was suggested for the customer and what he was paying for the items on it. He could take the product, install it for the customer, get his money, and not pay them until the end of the week. They would agree to give him the best cost possible and the best service by ordering anything he needed that they did not have in stock. If there was not an immediate need, he could call ahead, and they would drop it off as they went to other places in the area. They gave him a form to look at that he would agree to as he left with his parts.

Homer had spoken to the bank about the credit cards, and they wanted to do both on the day he got his loan for the building on Tuesday. He asked the banker about the gas contract and the new equipment, and the banker told him that they would consider that a sound investment in his future.

Homer and Alice were on their way to deliver the rabbit meat on Saturday, and they were discussing everything that had transpired this week. Homer said, "I can see that everyone will be depending on me to be an incredibly good bookkeeper instead of a mechanic. I will not be able to let more than a day go by without doing paperwork to survive. I am afraid of getting in over my head in paperwork."

Alice said, "I could do a lot of it every day after the library. I could prepare the deposit of the credit cards for both the bank and the gas company, so you could work more. I could also help you keep tract of the amounts owed to the parts store as well. We then can hire someone to keep our accounts for the government current and maybe even do our payroll. If that does not work, we could hire some younger person to pump gas and do odd jobs, so you can keep up with the paperwork. I believe in you, and I believe in us. I hope your mother has had a good week adjusting to the Mavis House since her move."

They arrived at the Mavis House to find his mother still in bed. Homer asked the attendant why that was and was told that she was refusing to get out of bed for them. She would slap at them with her good hand and not help in moving her to the chair. They said that they would try it again now he was there to visit her. Homer went into the room and gently lifted her from the bed to the chair and she did not resist. They applied support to help her stay in the chair and then left them alone for a while.

Homer said, "Momma is there a problem that you want to tell me about. Are you angry that I cannot take you home? I am deeply saddened by that fact momma, but I want what is best for you. I am running the garage now and I will own it on Tuesday. I could not work if you were at home. I would have to stay home and take care of you or hire someone to do it around the clock. I cannot afford to do that momma, or I would. We came by to tell you that we are getting married on the fifteenth of next month. We set the date the other night and we will be speaking to Alice's pastor today before we get home. I am going to see if they can take you to at least the wedding and bring you back after that. You are still a big part of my life and I do not want to worry that you are not working with the staff here to stay well."

There were tears forming on his momma's cheek as he spoke to her. She hung her head at the last comment and let go of his hand. Homer looked at her and saw a drool coming out of her mouth and he yelled for the staff. One of the nurses came right in and saw that Sis was not moving and looked as if she was having another stroke. They took her blood pressure, and it was extremely high again. They undid the restraints and placed her onto the bed as quickly as they could. Then they called for more help, and they had Homer and Alice follow someone out into the hall. In a couple of minutes, several of the people who had run into the room came walking out and Homer knew there was a problem. The head nurse that had come in first came out and spoke to them. She said, "I am sorry, but your momma just passed away. Can I call someone for you?"

Homer quietly said, "Would you call her brother Jake and

tell him about this."

Homer sat in a chair nearby and let the sobbing begin. Alice was holding him and crying herself as the staff offered them a room to go to for privacy. Jake was there in a few minutes and the four of them could go and see her one last time on the bed. To Homer she looked as if she was at peace now.

They did stop to see the pastor on the way home, but they did not meet on that day. Homer and Alice continued to the farm in silence and spent a quiet night together before Alice went home. She offered to stay on the couch, so he would not be alone, but Homer refused to have her do that. They did agree to go to Pastor Mike's service in the morning as she left for the night.

Homer thought it quite fitting to have Pastor Mike's sermon be about the peace a person would have known that we are going to be in heaven at the time of our death if we believed in Jesus during this lifetime. At the end of the service, Pastor Mike asked if there were people who wanted prayer before they went home. Homer and Alice went up to speak to him together. Homer said, "Pastor Mike, you told me the other day that you did not get to see me very often as we spoke of getting married. I know that, but you are the only church that momma and I ever attended that I could remember. I would like to ask you to do her funeral if you would."

Homer broke down and was crying again before Pastor Mike could say anything. He grabbed Homer by the shoulders and just hugged him as the tears flowed freely. Alice kept her hand on his back as the two men just stood there for a while. Pastor Mike said, "I would be honored to do the memorial service for your momma. Let me pray for you right now and you can come and see me tomorrow after work."

Homer and Alice had agreed to have dinner with her parents after the church service. Homer received the best wishes of her family and said they were praying for him to be at peace. They excused themselves shortly after dinner because they had not had any time to be with their aunt and uncle yet.

Jake and Flora were in the living room when they knocked on the door. They all greeted each other with a hug as they sat down together. Jake said, "I am glad that she was not alone when she died. It is surely a wonderful thing of Jesus to let you tell her about getting married and her meeting Alice. I did not get to see my mother alive after her stroke. They did not have the same medicines as they do now, and they could not get her blood pressure down. She never woke up like Sis did, so we could get to see her before she went to be with Jesus. I will check with the funeral home tomorrow and see if there are any plots left near our parents where we can let her rest. We can have the funeral on Wednesday or Thursday if you want. We still must go to the bank on Tuesday and finish that part of our lives as well. I know that my life will never be the same again after this week."

Homer said as he fought back the tears again, "I am glad

that I was there, and I know that it was nothing that anyone could have done any differently for her. The nurses came right in but this time it was over in a couple of minutes. Pastor Mike has agreed to do the funeral for us. I intended to speak to you about the offer from the oil company for the service station, but it doesn't seem that important now."

Jake shook his head and said, "Maybe it would be good for us to speak about something different for a little while. Did they offer you the new pumps like they did me? I wanted that to be your decision, but it sure sounded like a good thing to do. It seems to be a season of changes and a new face lift for the station is just one more thing changing. I would recommend you consider it at this time. Maybe they could do the work next month while you take your honeymoon."

The conversation remained lighter for a while and Flora made them a light supper before they left. Homer did check all the animals before they went into the house as he normally did. The two of them spent some time just holding onto each other before Alice went home for the night.

Homer called the gasoline rep in the morning and asked him if they could do the work as quickly as the fifteenth of next month if he was going to do it at all. He assured Homer that he would get the paperwork started right off and he would have an engineer come look at the yard as soon as possible. The rep asked him why the sudden hurry. Homer said, "My momma died on Saturday, and

I am getting married on the fifteenth of next month. I wasn't going to close the garage, but this would give me a chance to be away from work for a few days and I would like that now."

The rep lowered his voice as he said, "I am deeply sorry for the loss of your momma, and I will do all that I can to have the work started at that time. It takes about a week to dig up the old tanks and place the new ones with the canopy foundation having to be done at the same time. We will have you pumping gas in one week if everything goes well on the ground. We will do the outside work with you working there and it will not be a problem. I will call you as soon as I have anything to tell you. We will do this for you if we can."

Homer did go to the station on Monday, but it was extremely hard to do any work. He kept thinking about what had to be done. He did think to call his Uncle Stanley and tell him about his momma's death and when the funeral was going to be. His Uncle Jake had taken over the arrangements for his sister's funeral except for honoring Homer's wishes that Pastor Mike would do the service on Wednesday morning with the burial immediately following in the plot next to their parents.

The bank offered to postpone the closing for a couple of days, but it was held as scheduled. Homer got his credit card imprinter and his first book of deposit tickets to use with them at the same time. Homer told the banker that the work on the improvements to the station would be happening the following month starting on the fifteenth. Homer was going to own the first remodeled service station in the entire area with the company logo on the canopy for people to see. The bank lent him a promotional banner telling people that he was now taking credit cards at his station.

The funeral service was not overly well attended but Uncle Stanley did make it out and Homer was also able to invite him to the wedding the following month. People could see pictures of Molly Baker as she had been in life arrayed on the casket as Pastor Mike delivered her eulogy. He also told the people if they were not sure of where they would spend eternity that they could speak to him after the service. Homer sat stoically with Alice at his side in the front pew. Her parents had come to support them during this time. Her casket was taken to the cemetery and laid to rest near her parents. The women of the church had made a light lunch with lemonade for when it was all over, and they got to speak to some of their friends during that time. Homer was glad to be going back to the farm after it was all over. His being home early gave him a chance to do some work with the animals that he had delayed doing over the last few days.

Alice was spending the rest of the day with him, and she asked him to show her some of the farm as they took a walk. Homer first took her down the road to where the shack had been. He showed her the pile of ashes and the burned cook stove that had been their only source of heat as well as cooking range. They then circled around and went to the fields behind the house and sheds. They were seeing several animals as they walked including a white tail doe and fawn feeding. They flushed several rabbits and Alice kidded Homer on how he had not killed them all with his hunting.

Homer suspended his new sign telling people that he took credit cards for the purchases at his service station. He did not have a customer use one until the next day as the gasoline rep was there to speak to him. He did bring the forms and the contract as they had discussed last week. The rep said, "I had the engineer come here on Wednesday as you were closed and measure the yard and the street for his plan. He also took some measurements of the building and some photos from which to work from. I had to ask a couple of people to do me a favor to have the work started by the fifteenth, but it is all going to come together so that most of the work will be done while you are on your honeymoon. I know that this improvement will pay off in a big way for you and your new wife. Let us do a couple of these slips so you are sure how they work."

Homer had Ron come in from his bay to see how they had to be done and then he went back to work. Homer paid him for the gas that they had sold and then he went back to work. He had not made much money this week, but he knew that it was all going to work out.

Homer and Alice were keeping the appointment that they had delayed from the other day with her pastor. He did not ask the same questions of them that Pastor Mike had asked. He seemed to be concerned that the ceremony would be handled without any mistakes and being done on time. The pastor was telling them thank you and goodbye and Homer asked, "I guess you assume that we are ready to get married and that is why you have no questions for us."

The pastor got red in the face and said, "I do not know you, but I know Alice. I am sure that her parents have taught her what to expect from marriage and I let it go at that. You did not ask me for any counseling."

Homer said as he got up to leave, "I won't be asking you for any either." He took Alice by the hand and continued out the door with the pastor still sitting in his seat.

Alice said as they walked out of the church, "I guess I don't have to ask you whether you like our pastor. I am sure I will hear from my parents about this episode with him and I wonder how much of it will be the truth."

Homer and Alice were doing their Saturday delivery of rabbit meat. They left the restaurant and went to a store to buy some groceries for the house. It was on their way home that Homer drove to the cemetery and parked where he could view the fresh grave. Alice marveled at his words that he spoke, "Thank you Jesus for taking care of my momma."

Chapter Fifteen

It was raining by the time that they got back to the farm. Homer was angry with himself for not having all his rabbits under cover yet. He had two litters of young rabbits getting wet today. He made a promise to himself that he would get one built and become a better caretaker of his animals.

The two of them were sitting in the living room trying to decide where it would be best to keep the records of daily income from the service station when they heard a knock on the door. They had not heard anyone drive up, but the farmer and his wife were at the door. Homer opened the door and asked them to come in. He introduced everyone and then asked how he could help them. They had come over to tell them how sorry they were to hear of his momma's death. They had just been told and were sorry that they did not know in time to go to the funeral. Homer thanked them for their sentiments and asked them how they were doing this year with the crops. The farmer said he missed Homer's help, but his son was getting older and was starting to help around the farm. Homer asked him if he could hire him to spread the load of manure accumulating from the animals some day and the farmer told him he would be glad to do it for him. They spoke for a little longer and then they went home. On the way out the door, the farmer's wife said she was really going to miss the talks that she had with his momma.

Sunday morning found Alice and Homer at Pastor Mike's church service again. They were not aware as they went that it was potluck Sunday, and they were invited to stay and enjoy the fellowship of some of the other people at the church as well as the meal. They decided to stay and meet some of the other people and get to know them. They were invited to sit with Pastor Murray and his wife at their table. Homer got to tell him about the changes coming to the service station while they were going to be gone on their honeymoon. Homer asked him, "Pastor Mike, I have been thinking about the questions you asked us about our getting married. Alice's pastor only told us to not be late and I don't understand the differences I see in the two of you."

Pastor Mike said, "I really do not know Alice's pastor much more than I know Alice. I take the position in life to try and find out what a person knows about themselves and about Jesus. It is my job in a way to teach you how much Jesus loves us while we are here on this earth. I may go to your service station to get my car worked on, but you do not know what to fix if you do not ask me first. I want to know if there is anything in your life that I can fix so you can go to heaven and be with Jesus when you die. I also want you to know how he cares for us every day of our lives. That is why I ask questions."

Alice spoke up and said, "My pastor tells us what not to do on a regular basis, but you seem to tell people what we must do for Jesus and how to recognize His love for us. I feel that after listening to you about what I need to do that I automatically know what I cannot do. I sometimes wonder how often we are told that we are bad people in our church and left with no hope of ever being good enough. You let people know of God's love as a gift and we do not have to earn His love by not doing something out of fear. As a little girl, I was loved by my parents after having been a bad girl in some way. You make God sound like a loving Father and He really does not get angry every time we do something wrong. I understand that there are some things in our lives that he does not want us to do and over time we usually get better at living and not doing those things. You made it sound as if God took Sis right to heaven and cradled her in His arms when she got there."

Pastor Mike said, "I don't know if it is exactly like that, but I believe that it is something genuinely like that as we get to heaven. Jesus died on the cross to forgive our sins at Calvary. If we believe that Jesus is the Son of God and believe that He forgives our sins when we ask Him, He is faithful and true to forgive them. Many times, in the bible it tells us to go and sin no more after our forgiveness. Do you have that assuredness, Alice?"

Alice shyly responded, "I know who Jesus is and the story about His life. I know he did many miracles while He was on earth. I try to not sin, but I do not know if I have ever asked Jesus to forgive my sins in that manner."

Pastor Mike felt obliged to ask, "Would you like to ask Him now, so you too could be assured of going to heaven someday. We could pray together here or in a quieter room in the back. Homer can come with us."

The three of them went to a quiet room and prayed together as Pastor Mike led them. Alice stood beside Homer and the tears started streaming down her face as she prayed the sinner's prayer. When they were finished praying and Alice had composed herself, they went back out to join the others in fellowship. On the way out of the room, Alice looked at Pastor Mike and said, "I wish we had asked you to do our wedding as well as the funeral. Please forgive us for that."

Pastor Mike simply told her that there was, nothing to forgive and he wished them both the best that Jesus could bless them with.

On Monday Homer decided to move the sign advertising about the acceptance of credit cards to the side of the building toward the main street. If the gas customers were going to keep him interrupted from his work, he was going to have to pump a lot more gas. Homer signed a soft contract with the parts dealer down the street as well for the time that he was going to be on his honeymoon. The parts people knew Ron and Homer told them he could sign for parts if he was not around. They were going to give him a bill on Friday, and he was to bring in a check for the full amount on Monday and the week would start over.

Many of the nights recently had been spent discussing the

different aspects of their wedding. Alice had stayed in town a couple of nights to work on invitations and things like that with her mother. One night the two of them were discussing where they would go on their honeymoon and they both liked the thought of going to the ocean shore and seeing what that was like. Jake had told Homer that he would work at the station during the week that they were gone and help to see to the work and try to keep the garage side open for work. He was also going to feed the animals that week. Homer was going to hold back the breeding of a couple of does so he would not have too many rabbits come to the right weight while he was gone. He had also arranged for the restaurant to accept twenty rabbits and freeze some of them until he got home. Homer was starting to feel like most things were covered in the plan.

It was the night before their wedding and Alice and Homer were trying to have a couple of minutes in private. There had been little of that in the last few days. There were people measuring out where they would dig at the service station next week. Uncle Jake had come by to get an idea of what it was going to be like and how to do the new credit card deposits for the bank. Alice had talked to the flower shop, the cake maker, dress seamstress, and everyone else who had a part in the wedding. Homer asked, “Are you sorry that you said yes?”

Alice angrily said, “You better be careful, or I will beat you with a sharp stick like your sharp tongue. My love grows for you every day and I cannot wait until I no longer go home at night from your house. I am going to bring a couple of boxes of my clothes over to your house before the wedding, so I will have some clothes when we get back from the ocean."

Alice was interrupted by the ringing of the telephone. Her mother answered it and then she was heard gasping, and she handed the receiver to Mr. Moodie. They were all standing by waiting to hear what the commotion was all about. Mr. Moodie hung up the phone and faced them with a weird look on his face and said, "Pastor has fallen and is in the hospital with a broken leg. He will not be able to do the ceremony for you tomorrow, but he was quick to suggest another pastor doing it in his church. I now must call that pastor and see if he will do it for us on such a short notice."

Alice held up her hand to stop her father and said, "Daddy, I would like to call Homer's pastor first if we can't have our own. I am sure that if we can find him that he would do it for us. May we call him first please?"

The telephone rang as Pastor Mike was starting to prepare for bed. He got up and said hello. He heard, "Hello Pastor Mike, this is Alice Moodie. I am sorry to call you so late, but we have an emergency of sorts."

Pastor Mike asked, "What kind of an emergency is this, Alice?"

Alice continued, "We just got a call from our pastor, and he has fallen. He is currently in the hospital with a broken leg and cannot not do our ceremony tomorrow. He suggested another pastor use his church for the ceremony, but I would like to have you do it. I know that Homer would agree because he only let me have all the say in the wedding planning, but I believe Jesus knows best. Would you marry us in my church tomorrow please?"

Pastor Mike said, "I would be honored to do it for you. I do not really know the layout of your church, but I will come early and get myself familiar with it and any equipment we may be using. I will meet someone there in the morning. Good night."

Alice turned to the rest of the people and said it was all settled and that Pastor Mike was going to do the ceremony. He only needs to get in a little early to see the layout and any equipment he will be using. Alice could see the big smile on Homer's face as she told them and the seriousness on her father's face.

Homer was as nervous as he had ever felt when he got up in the morning. He had cleaned up and was trying to get into the suit that he had bought to get married in. He went to see if his uncle knew how to tie a tie because he had never worn one in his life. It was his aunt that finally helped him tie it. Homer did not know anything about tradition, so he had asked his uncle to be the best man for the wedding. His uncle had told him how it was usually a younger person or at least nearer his age but he had not wavered in his request. At last, the final preparations were made, and they left for the church with the rings in his uncle's pocket.

The ceremony went off without too much laughter, but it was done in taste by Pastor Mike in the way that he orchestrated what had to be done. He had Homer and Alice up on the small stage, so they could be seen and photographed by their family and friends. He gave a short teaching on what the wedding bands represent with the endless circle of love and then finished the vows. He then pronounced them man and wife and told Homer to kiss his wife for the first time. The two of them went to the back of the church for some extra photographs to be taken and then moved to the reception area in the basement of the church.

Homer finally took the time to look at some of the people who had attended their wedding. His Uncle Stanley and most of his family had come as well as Ron the mechanic. He would have to be introduced to most of the rest of her relatives and friends. They took a place at the head table and in a few minutes the line of people who wanted to greet them started. They were not half done the line when it was time for the food to be served. They were allowed a few minutes to eat before the line started back up again. One of the first one to come in the line was Pastor Mike. He took a minute and blessed them again as he told them he had to leave. Alice gave him a special hug and a big thank you as he left.

They did a few more traditional things such as cutting the cake and opening a few of the gifts before they left for the ocean. Uncle Jake was going to move the presents to the house after the wedding was finished. As they were leaving, her mother came over to see Alice and she was crying as she said goodbye. Homer noticed that there was an exchange during the hugging, but he did not know what it was.

Homer's car had been packed the day before for the honeymoon. He even put in a couple of emergency tools in case of some minor problems. They had called in a reservation for a nice motel that was about halfway to the ocean where they planned to stay the first night. He had brought a bag with some casual clothing, so he did not have to travel in his suit and changed in a room at the church and had his uncle take the suit to the farm as well. They had to pull away from the last of the people that were still hanging around as they finally left. Homer got into the car after he had opened the door for Alice and asked if Mrs. Baker was ready to go to the ocean with her husband. He only got a kiss for an answer.

It took three hours of traveling to reach the motel for the night. On the way, Alice said, "My mother gave us this without my father knowing about it." She reached into a pocket and came out with one hundred dollars. I thanked her for us but please do not ever mention it again. They each took a bag and went into the office to get their room. It was on the second floor, and they were told it would not get the early morning sun, so they could stay in bed longer. They walked up the stairs together to see where they would become man and wife in a different way. Homer was the first to use the shower and then came back to the room in his underwear. Alice then got up and brought a small bag into the bathroom with her and she whispered in Homer's ear that he should lose the underwear before she came back out.

Homer was surprised as he woke up and looked at the clock in the room and saw how late it was. He reached out and found that it had not been a dream and he was really in bed with his wife. He turned over in bed and watched her sleep for a few minutes but then decided he should wake her up in a special way. She was drowsy at first but was soon responding to her husband.

They showered one more time before they went out to find some breakfast and headed for the shore. They took their time as they traveled and reached the shore in plenty of time to see the sunset from their motel room. The brilliant colors of the rainbow displayed in the spray of a wave crashing on a nearby rock formation on the shore added to the beauty of the scene. The white sand was seen ending at this vast expanse of water with no end except for the horizon hanging above it. Homer said, "I never thought to wonder what the ocean would look like. I can see the beauty that many people see in it, but I can also sense the need to give it respect because of how unending it is. I think I prefer the forests where I can plant my feet on solid ground."

Alice looked at him, "Okay, on our next honeymoon we will go to the mountains for your choice. Thank you for letting me see something I have wanted to see for a long time as I grew up and read about it in books. Now I have a memory that I do not have to depend on someone else to tell me about in a book."

The days flew by, and they enjoyed new mysteries of the ocean and then had to return home to reality. Homer said, “I have not thought about the service station all week. See how you distract me every day as Mrs. Baker. I now need to go home and remember everything that you helped me forget for one week.”

Alice kissed him as she asked, “Will you remember this week as fondly as I will? I am going to cherish these memories for the rest of my life. You say that you had never thought about what an ocean would look like, but I never thought about what marriage would look like. The dreams that are found in a book have nothing to compare to being in your arms and feeling you close to me.”

They kissed a long lingering kiss before finishing up their packing to go home. Homer drove a little faster and they made it back to the farm in one long day on the road. It was not too late as they drove by his uncle’s house, so he blew the horn on the way by. They walked into the darkening rooms of the farmhouse and Alice said, “I don’t have to drive home tonight because I am already home.”

Chapter Sixteen

Homer arrived at the station at the usual time to open. He was not totally prepared to see the station in such disarray. There were piles of dirt in the front and barricades warning people to stay back from the holes. There were pipes sticking out of a cement pad where they said the pumps would be in the drawings. There were two large steel posts sticking out of the concrete that were for the canopy. There was what could be seen of one large tank and one smaller one that was going to be for the new gas called Hi-Test with more octane than the regular gas, whatever octane was. Homer had been told that the car companies were making cars that ran better on the Hi-Test and he was one of the first stations in his area to have it available. He had to wonder if he had sold his soul to the devil with this deal.

Ron came in a few minutes later and said hello to Homer. Homer asked him if there was any work that was waiting, and he was told that there were two customers coming in this morning. Ron said, "You need to be careful when you bring a car around but there is still room to get in and your uncle did the paperwork for last week. He told me to tell you that he would be in before noon today."

They were still talking when the crew that was putting in the tanks and new pumps started to arrive. One of them came over and asked if Homer was home yet. Homer acknowledged him and asked him what he wanted.

The man said, “We need to dig some trenches to get the electricity to the new pumps from the building. We dig them and install some conduit in which to run wires in later and then we fill the holes back in. I would like to do it around the middle of the morning, and we will not leave tonight until the trenches are filled again. Let me show you where we must go, and you can decide if today is okay.”

The two men walked outside as the first customer arrived for the morning work. They had to dig in front of one of the bays where he usually worked but it would be easier today than tomorrow because of more work coming in for the morning. The next problem was where they came into the building behind the front door, and they would have to open that area as well. Homer had to remind the man about the new front to the building and asked if it would interfere with any portion of that. The man had to admit that he did not have the plans and he would give the man at the company a call immediately to find out. It turned out that it was not going to interfere with any of that, so they could go ahead as soon as Homer had the car out of the bay they were going to block.

Jake came by late in the morning and the digging was already happening by the bay. They were bringing in sand to pack around the tanks and all the lines that were buried in the ground. The metal fill brackets were being installed for the tanker trucks and they were going to pour the last of the cement later in the day.

It looked like a swarm of bees working out there at times. The men had to hurry because the first load of gasoline was scheduled in the morning and then the pumps were going to be set. An electrician would wire the pumps and switches in the morning as well. They told Homer that he would be pumping gas on Wednesday as soon as the state monitored the pumps for accuracy. The canopy was going to come in on a truck and set by crane at a future date. The poles were standing erect from their cement bases already. The people who would be doing the face lift on the service station would be coming in separately after they were gone.

Jake asked Homer if he had enjoyed where they had been on their honeymoon. Homer assured him it was a wonderful place to visit but he liked his feet on solid ground. His uncle just laughed. Homer got the papers for last week and went to the parts store as agreed.

Homer wanted to get home before dark today, so he could see the new rabbit shed that a customer had built while he was gone. He did not want any of his rabbits in the rain or the sun if he could help it and this shed was going to allow that for as many rabbits as he had now. He had it built with two ends open for the summer and he could tarp areas closed for the winter. He also had a room added in the middle for starting chicks out of the weather. It was exceptionally low profile, and you opened the coop from the top to work with the chicks. These hatches could be left open in the summer heat and wire placed over them to contain the chicks. It was big enough to keep fifty chicks for up to six weeks and then move them to a bigger coop. He was going to get some new laying chicks in a few days. The other thing that the man did was to bury some wire and pipes, so he could have lights and fresh water at the coops. The last thing that the man did was to separate the original coop into two parts with a removable wall of fencing, so he could get the laying chicks started with some hens still laying eggs.

On their first evening home together, Alice took a piece of paper and wrote down the gifts they had opened already and who they were from. Then they opened the last of their gifts and prepared to write thank-you cards for the donors. Alice had to tell Homer what some of the gifts were when they received several gadgets for the kitchen including an electric blender. The new dish set for eight was done in a country setting with animals and fields. They also received some blankets and what Homer called useless knick-knacks for the house. What Homer liked best was the toaster that did two slices of bread.

Alice finished her list and then they went upstairs for the night. Homer suddenly realized that his room was now quite small. He stated to Alice that he would move them to the bigger room that used to belong to his momma as soon as he could get her things out of there. He asked her to help him figure out if some of the things could be donated or if they were to simply be discarded. Alice asked him, "Would you like to have a different bed for us? I have some money that we could use for a new bed if you would like.

You have never asked me to pay for anything, but I have been working for a long time and I have some money set aside for such a time as this."

Homer defiantly said, "If you have some money, it belongs to you, and you can do what you want to with it."

Alice was quick to correct him, "What I had is ours now. We became one when we married. I would like a new bed for us, but you must want it also or I can't do it."

Homer agreed, "I know that we became one. This is more of that stuff that I do not know how to do while I am around other people. I would like it if we got a new bed, and we can go shopping on Saturday as I deliver the rabbit meat. That will give me time to clean out the room for us. I must kill some chickens as well as some rabbits this week. I suppose that I should show you something and you can help me learn some more." He went to a corner of the kitchen and got out a can marked for flour and brought it out for her. He started to explain as he opened it, "Momma and I never used a bank until I worked for Uncle Jake, and we still did not put our extra money in the bank. I just put it in there and momma would buy food and things that we needed as it came up. I have been putting some in there since I started working for Uncle Jake and I really do not know how much I have." He emptied the contents on the table and then they sorted and counted it up. He had over two thousand dollars in that can when they finished. Alice just looked at him with a strange smile on her face.

Alice said, "I think that we should find a better place for some of this money. I think we should invest some as well as keep a little nest egg in a bank where we can get it quickly. Do you know what I mean when I say that we should invest some of it?" Homer shook his head no and she continued, "It is where you put your money with a company for interest. A bank pays you interest on the money you keep in a savings account. They charge you interest on the money they lend you like what you borrowed to buy the service station. A bank always charges you more interest than they pay you and that is how they stay in business. There are other companies who pay more interest than banks because they use their money to buy big companies. They let lots of people who give them money to buy the companies receive a share of the profits that the company makes. You then have the option of leaving that money on deposit and they will reinvest that money for you and pay you a bigger share of the profits. People who do this usually do better than just putting your money in a bank. You borrowed money to buy the service station, so you pay interest to a bank and then you can keep the profits for yourself. These companies do not borrow money but use yours and other people to buy these companies and you get a share of the profits without paying the banks their interest. Do you understand some of what I just said?"

Homer seemed to be thinking hard, "I think I do but we can go over it again another day. What I did hear you say is the way to make the most money is to own the business and owe no debt. I owe no debt to the animals so that is all profits. I need to pay back my bank before I get to keep all the profits but owning it is still better than working for someone. Who do we speak to about investing money like you say or are there ways to make one of our businesses pay us more profits?"

Alice chided, "Do I hear some greediness in those words or are you trying to use the wisdom that God gave you? I believe that you will make a good living with the service station, and we will make enough to pay for things in the house with the animals. That is what you told me that you wanted to have when we were still going out together."

Homer calmly said, "I remember and that is still true. I just do not want us to have needs that we can not pay for. I will never forget those years. Why don't we go to bed for the night after we put this back and spend some time together?"

The workers had done as they said they would do. The yard at the service station was nicely filled in and they had barricades around the drying cement. They could pull vehicles right into the bays with no trouble and the gasoline was delivered as expected. The pumps came in the back of another truck and an electrician was doing a lot of wiring in the back room. Homer was joking with the lead foreman and told him he thought that he was going to have to go to another station to get gasoline for his car. The man assured him that he would be pumping gasoline before the end of the day tomorrow if he could wait.

Alice and Homer were having dinner with her parents that night. Her mother wanted to hear about the trip and what they thought of the ocean. They were eating their dinner when Alice asked her father if he had ideas as to whom to invest with. He told them that there was a good investment firm in the next town, and it had a good record of returns for their people. He asked them why she had asked. She kept her answer vague but told him that the banks were not paying enough now. She spoke of her money with no amount mentioned but added that she wanted to contribute as much as she could to their welfare. Her father complimented her on her idea and gave her the name of a representative that he knew personally. The rest of the evening was all small talk relating to the things they had seen in the ocean.

Homer felt like a new parent the next day as he pulled his car over to the pumps and got some gasoline pumped into his car. The workers were prepared and put a banner across the yard that said Homer was open for business again. The company rep was going to move it in a week or so to another station. It was good to have his old clients able to come back and get their gas again. Homer was amazed at how many new customers were stopping now with the new pumps and taking credit cards. The new canopy had been delivered and put up the following Tuesday with the company logo facing the street. It had its own internal lighting system if you wanted to be open earlier or later when it was dark outside. He was also the only station in town where the customers were not out in the rain.

Pastor Mike stopped by one day to see how things were going. Homer and Alice were going to church more regularly now, and they had asked him to stop by and see the changes. He also had a young man with him and came into the office to ask Homer a question. Pastor Mike said, "I would like you to meet my young friend Frank Perkins. You and he have a lot in common in your past. For a long time, he did not go to school and has only recently learned how to read or write a lot. He is particularly good with numbers and is very honest. He is also from one of the poorest families in the area. I wondered if you could use him to pump gas for you and you could teach him more because he loves cars. He is even willing to pump gasoline on a Saturday if your company ever decides you must for them."

Homer looked at the young man who was looking back at him. He said, "They are already asking me to pump gasoline at least for part of Saturday since the remodeling. You say he is good with numbers and is honest with people and I would need to know that was true to hire him. How would you get to work if I hired you and are you done with school yet?"

Frank said, "I do not live that far from here and could walk most days. I am not in a regular school but go to some classes held at night for adults who need help. You could count on me to be here on time and to be honest with your customers."

They spoke for a few more minutes and Homer agreed to give the young man a try. Pastor Mike thanked him and congratulated him on the new work at the station. Homer then told him that they were coming back to put a new exterior on the building with more logos on it. Homer even told him that he was seriously considering putting in hydraulic lifts, so they could work under a car standing up. Pastor Mike said he was not sure what they were going to come up with next.

Alice and Homer had bought a new bed and moved into the downstairs bedroom. They had discussed a few other things about the layout of the rooms in the house and had made some other changes to suit Alice. Homer was now delivering meat to two restaurants on a regular basis. He was making use of the four coops and had been able to continue to sell eggs as well as what they used. They had enough chickens that his uncle and he could have all the chicken meat they wanted and had given some to Frank and his family as well.

Frank was proving to be a great asset to the garage. He was a quick learner and was incredibly good with numbers. He would smile most of the day long as he waited on people and served them. He took an interest in learning the mechanical side of the station as well when he was not pumping gasoline. The help was especially appreciated as they changed the outside of the building as they had promised within the next month after the pumps were installed. Once Homer was comfortable with his work, they started to pump gas on Saturday mornings. They were now selling enough gasoline that the truck had to stop more than once a week for a delivery.

Homer and Frank were in the office shortly after he had started to work, and Homer asked him about his family and why he had not gone to school.

Frank answered, "I usually don't speak about my family to anyone, but I don't think you are asking so that you can make fun of me, so we can talk about some of it. I am one of six children. I think the thing that my father is best at is having children, so he can play with them. He seems to have trouble keeping a job that pays all our bills. Do not get me wrong. He is a good worker but quite uneducated and that did not bother him much. He did not care if I went to school, and I never really liked being around some of the other kids when they picked on our clothes or our not having shoes. It was not until I started to get into fights as a teen that I really found a desire to learn a better way. I was a good fighter but that never seemed to make me any friends or improve how my life was going. There was always someone waiting to pick a fight around the next corner. I had just finished a fight when this man came over to me and asked me if I was happy that I was fighting. We got to talking and I found out that he was a pastor, and we became friends. He came to see me at my house and never once made fun of us. He never seemed to be doing anything bossy, but I was soon in classes and now I am working for you. I do not want to let him down in anything that I do."

Homer said, "No wonder Pastor Mike said you had a life like mine. Someday I will tell you part of my story, but life can become what you make of it with your decisions. You will never become sorry for the right decision, but you can pay a lifetime for the wrong one. Did you hear that we are going to put in a hydraulic lift in one bay to try it?"

The small talk was ended by customers coming for gasoline, but Homer knew that he wanted to know this young man better. He asked Alice before he did it, but he took Frank out to the farm one day to see the animals. He studied all the pens and coops while asking how it all worked. They all had a meal together before Homer brought him home for the night.

The people from the car parts store that Homer did most of his buying from were helping him buy the lift on time payments and they were installing it as agreed. They were all learning how to put their arms under the cars and where it was safe to lift from. The lift had to carry the frame of the cars for it to be safe to be under them. Homer and Ron were fascinated at seeing the bottom of a car while standing under it. They could do so much of the work that they had been crawling under the cars for while standing up and movement was much quicker. They also found that it was easier to do some things that were hard while on your back. They could take off all four tires and change them from one lift and not pull a jack all around the floor of the garage. Even his Uncle Jake was impressed when he saw it work for the first time.

Homer’s Shack

Chapter Seventeen

Homer could do most of the bookkeeping during slow times and once Frank arrived for the day. Alice would stop by on the way home from the library and would often help get the deposit slips organized. They were now doing a lot of business with credit cards, and they had to be recorded on a deposit slip individually for the bank or the gas company. Homer noticed that Alice seemed tired in the afternoon for a week. He asked her about it, and she made light of it and went about her work. She seemed all right to him, so he let it go. The next morning as they got up to go to work, he noticed that she was not having coffee or eating breakfast. His uncle stopped by that day and Homer spoke to him about it. His uncle advised him to have her go to a doctor right away and Homer asked him why. Jake said, "I think that I am about to teach you something new again today. You have never been around enough people to know that a woman who is expecting a child is often sick in the morning for the first few months of her pregnancy. I believe that you are about to become a daddy."

Alice arrived at the office in the afternoon and Homer had her get into his car without telling her why. He drove her to the doctor's office, and she started to argue about not needing to go in. Homer said, "I really don't know much about a lot of things, but I want to know that you are all right. I had someone tell me that the symptoms you are displaying could be because you are about to become a momma. I want you to see the doctor and we can both be sure what we need to do from now on."

Homer walked in with her, and she was taken to the examination room by a nurse. The same nurse came and got Homer in a little while and asked him to come back to the room with them. The doctor told them that she was to have her baby in about seven months by what she had told him. He gave them a book on diet and spoke about a few things they needed to look for that things were going okay. They both thanked the doctor, and they walked out to the car together. Alice got into the middle as usual and gave Homer a kiss before they drove back to the station.

Alice was stern as she spoke, "I was certain that I was going to have a baby before today. I do not want you to make a big deal out of this because women have babies all the time. I do not want to tell my parents until I feel it is the right time and I am going to work if I can before I give up my job at the library. I will be able to help you with the bookkeeping right up to the day that I have the baby. I know that you will make a great daddy. I will help you understand some of the things that will happen to me as they get closer to the time."

They arrived back at the station and they both went back to work as if nothing had happened. Alice left in a few minutes to go and prepare the meal for tonight.

Homer went to care for the animals as he usually did when

he arrived home. He lingered with the chickens and the rabbits as his troubled mind tried to grasp what was happening. He was going to be a father. He loved to play with children, but he had never had to care for one, especially one of his own. He lingered to the point that Alice called him to say that his meal was ready. He turned out the lights in the coop and went into the house.

Alice asked if there was some trouble in the coops or if he was just out there thinking. Homer answered, "You may already know me too well. I was out there thinking about our day and our future. I have never had to take care of children in my life, and I have only known a few. I do not mean to say that I am not happy that you are pregnant because I had a part to do with that. I was nervous trying to learn how to be around you and now I will have to care of a child without looking totally stupid."

"I thought we were getting to the part where you thought you are stupid," Alice said sharply. "We will do the same thing we have done right along. We will learn how to care for our child, and we will love him or her very much. You will make a great father and you will give me whatever help I need when the time comes. Your supper is getting cold so go ahead and eat."

Jake stopped by the next day to find out if he had been right. Homer told him he was right, but they were not telling anyone just yet and asked him to keep it a secret. Jake laughed when he said that a lot of people would know in less than nine months.

Homer and Alice were stopping by her parents on the way home from the garage a couple of nights later. They had decided that they were sure enough of what they were doing and how they felt that they could go and see what her parents would think of becoming grandparents. They did not even want to go into the living room but met her parents at the kitchen nook where they would eat their meals together. Alice said, "Mom and Dad, I wanted you to know that I have not been feeling well for a couple of months and we have not been over here as much as we could have. Homer is doing very well at the garage and must spend a lot of time there also. I went to see the doctor the other day because the illness seemed to linger longer than it should. He ran some tests and said that I should feel a lot better in about seven months."

Her mother did not let her finish the sentence before she had Alice sit down and rest in a chair. They both said that they felt wonderful at the thought of becoming grandparents while they were still young enough to enjoy a child's energy. Homer finally let down his guard and allowed a smile to come over his face with their enthusiasm. Her father slapped him on the shoulder and congratulated him. Her sister who came in during the conversation gave her a big hug and asked if she could tell their brother to which they said yes. The chores at home were going to be done late tonight.

Homer had been doing very well at the service station and he and Alice decided they could go and see the investor that they had used when they had put the two thousand dollars to work. They wanted to see how their investments were doing and maybe add some to the total. The riding was becoming a little more comfortable for Alice as she was nearly over the morning nausea. They were greeted warmly by a receptionist who asked whom they were there to see. They were then invited to sit as she went to get the man. The man came back with her and greeted them. They were brought back to an office, and he asked what he could do for them.

Homer said, "We came by to get some idea if we had chosen the right stocks to invest in and possibly change our choices as well as add some more to the total. I believe that we bought stocks in Coca Cola and the oil company I sell gas for."

The man walked over to a file and brought out a folder with their names on it before sitting down again. He said, "You have not had your investment with me for long, but you will see that there has been some growth to those you chose. You must have bought the Coca Cola at just the right time because it has already split once. What that means is the company likes to keep the price of their shares lower at times. The company will take the profits that you would normally receive as a dividend and create a duplicate stock with each having more than half the value of one. This is not the real value but if your stock were selling for ten dollars, the company would give you two stocks valued at five dollars and twenty-five cents. This keeps it so more people will invest in the lower priced stocks. You saw a nice gain in value at that point and it is still rising. The oil company stock has risen over two percent in the time it has been invested. You do understand that the stock market is best utilized if you leave your money in it for a long time and that is what you told me you wanted."

Homer explained, "That is what we want, and we are certainly glad to hear that our money is growing. We have other things that are growing, and I want to be sure that my family is cared for in the future. My uncle mentioned what he called quarter stocks that he has done well in. What can you tell us about those kinds of investments?"

The man said, "Those stocks are usually from companies that are just trying to get started. They offer a lot of people chances to come in and help them grow. They are often in technology fields where there is not always a product but an idea for a product. They do not cost much and those who succeed do well and those who go bust are just that. We have several available now and we can discuss some of them if you would like."

The discussion led Homer and Alice to keep most of their money they were going to add to the oil company stock. They did take forty dollars and invested in two start-up stocks. One stock was called Cabella's who were starting a sporting goods store and the other was Texas Instruments who were creating handheld electronics.

Homer was lying in bed with his arm across his wife and

patting her now slightly bulging stomach. Homer asked, "Is there anything that you need me to do for you or the baby that I am not aware of? Are you sure that you want to continue to work the entire time, or do you want to get things ready before you have the baby?"

Alice's answer was curt, "You are so good to me and the baby. I have everything that I need now. I expect that my mom or sister will give me a baby shower in a couple of months, and we will have most of the things we will need for the house at that time. The house needs little work, and we will move the furniture as the day gets closer. As far as work goes, I like what I do, and I do not want to start lying around the house when I can be around people. I told my mother and father that if they wanted to see their grandchild they would eventually have to come to our house. I am getting angry that they do not come here to visit but expect us to go to their house all the time. Not one of my friends has come out to see me since I was married except at work. I guess we could have originated the visits to their house and maybe they would be more comfortable coming to our home. It is not nice to feel lonely in a crowd of people. I'm sorry for saying that but I did not think all my friends would leave me because I got married."

Homer tried to comfort her, "I think I know what you mean. I see people every day, but I do not have anyone that I consider a friend. There were many years that I did not want people to know about me and momma, but I have worked hard to get this service station up and going and there is no one to talk to about it. We may have to work together at meeting with some of your friends to start with and see what happens from there. I do not want you to be lonely. You can go without me if you want to."

Alice snapped back, "If my friends do not want to see the both of us, they are not my friends at all. There would be no reason for me to go alone except while you are at work, and I do not want to go without you. Maybe there are people in the church that we could meet and visit if our friends no longer want to be around us. We are never alone if we know Jesus as we do."

Homer patted her on the belly a couple more times and then kissed her good night. He made one more comment as he rolled over about what they were going to name their baby. Alice said that would have to wait for another time because she was tired.

Uncle Jake and Aunt Flora had planted a few vegetables in the plot that they had gotten ready for Sis. They were out there on an early Saturday morning as Homer went out to slaughter the rabbits for delivery. Jake asked how things were going with the baby. Homer admitted that Alice was lonely for her friends but things with the baby were going well. Flora offered to stop by and see her and Homer thanked her for the gesture. Homer asked them if they needed some of the meat in the freezer and they said no. Jake asked if he could tend the heifers and all the chickens the following week. They were going to take a train ride to another city and stay there for a few days seeing the sights. Homer told him that it would be no problem.

Homer left Alice at the house to rest as he went to deliver the rabbits later that morning. On the way back, he stopped to see how Frank was doing at the service station. As Homer turned into the lot, he could see two cars at the pumps and one more waiting as Frank was hurrying back and forth. Homer asked him if he needed a hand and Frank asked him to run a credit card for him, so he could watch another pump. Homer took the money from a couple of the customers as Frank continued to fill up the waiting cars. It was the time that Frank usually stopped pumping gas, but the cars kept coming. He wanted to do as much as he could for Homer so they both stayed working until they got caught up and then they closed for the day. Homer asked, "Is it usually like this on a Saturday morning or is this unusual?"

Frank was short of breath as he answered, "The last two weeks have been like this. There was a man who wanted a flat tire fixed today but I just did not have time to do it. He left it and asked if he could pick it up around noon on Monday. I put his name on it and left it in the shop. I am glad you are here because I don't like to leave this much money in the garage unattended over the weekend."

Homer gathered up the credit card receipts and the money in the drawer and put them in a bag to take home. They locked up the station and Homer gave Frank a ride home. Homer said, "Have I told you how good a job you have been doing for me? Are you still interested in becoming a mechanic or do you have other dreams?"

Frank answered, "I like working on cars and I like working for you. Ron has let me do some things for him when you are not around to help him. I know how to do tire repairs and some simple things like that. Why do you ask?"

"I may get someone else for you to train to pump gas, so you do not have to work as hard on a Saturday," Homer answered. "That would give us time to teach you more about the mechanical side of the service station. Alice is getting tired with all the hours she is putting in and I want to do most of the bookkeeping during the day, so we do not have to do it while she could be resting. We now have the two lifts, and they were well worth the money. I have my eye on some air tools to make the work even faster for us. I do not mind hard work, but I do not want to be stupid about how we do things. They say you can take a tire off in less than a minute with these new tools once the car is in the air."

They had gotten to Frank's home and were sitting in the driveway by this time. Two of his siblings were playing ball in the yard and waved as he was pulling out again. He was now late for doing his chores at the farm. He took the money into the house and asked Alice what she might have for lunch. He then went out and got all the animals fed and the eggs put away for the day. When he got back to the house, there was a sandwich and soup ready on the table and Alice was making some of the deposits. Alice said, "Frank must have been busy all morning because there are a lot of cards and quite a lot of cash today. Did you get to speak to him today about maybe hiring him some help like we discussed?"

Homer said, "I talked to him as I drove him home. He was so busy that when I went to pick up the deposits, he still had four cars in the lot and two more came before we could close and leave. I took some of the money as he pumped the gas. He still wants to become a mechanic and I think he will be good at it. Did you get some rest like you were supposed to? I see that the floor in the living room has been mopped."

Alice sputtered, "I cannot just sit around the house like you think I should. I am pregnant but most of the women in the world still can work during their pregnancies. That is why I do not want to quit my job yet. You would have me sitting around and getting lazy."

They talked back and forth as they got the deposit ready. Homer told her how concerned he was about her health and wanted her and the baby to be well as possible. Alice continued to assure him that she and the baby were doing well, and he did not have to worry. They were so busy that they did not notice the car pulling up to the house until there was a knock on the door.

Homer went to the door and was met my Alice's parents. Homer welcomed them into the house as Alice gathered up the receipts and deposited money they were working on. Her father tried to make a joke about the king in his counting room counting all his money. Alice welcomed him with a kiss on the cheek and told him it was all part of the job and not the king's ransom they were dealing with. Her mother came in and waited until Alice had come over to see her. Alice said, "Come on you two let us show you our home with no notice that you were coming."

The house was described to her parents as they walked around. Homer was now glad that his wife had washed the dining room floor where he had dripped some blood from the rabbit meat earlier in the day. It was a beautiful day, so they went onto the back porch to sit as they overlooked the back of the farm. Homer served them some sun tea they had made earlier as they sat around and chatted. Alice's mother said, "At least my grandchild will have plenty of room to run in. You have a wonderful place here with all this land away from the cars."

Alice made a jab at her mother as she said, "I'm glad you approve now you have finally come out to see where we live. Should I get some more chicken from the freezer, so you can eat with us?"

Her father answered, "I don't think we will be staying that long. We came to apologize for not having come out here before now, but we want to let you rest before you go to work on Monday. Are you planning to work as long as you can?"

Alice's voice rose as she said, "Is this a conspiracy between you and my husband? I know that I do not have to work but I want to. I could not stay home all week and not do anything. I will probably stay home and get the house ready near my delivery date but that is all I am planning for now."

Her mother said, "I know that you will be fine, and it was just a question and not part of an interrogation. We both would be more comfortable if you had a telephone installed in your home in case of an emergency. We are concerned for you and the baby to be well. Would you be interested in using some of the baby things we still have like the crib or are you going to get different ones?"

Alice answered, "I haven't even thought that far ahead yet, but we probably should get a phone in here to help with the business as well. I will ask Homer what he would like to do as far as baby things, and we will get back to you soon. Thanks for offering and thanks for your concern but I am doing well."

A few minutes later, her parents left, and the rest of the weekend became theirs again. They attended Pastor Mike's church the next day and made a point of speaking to some of the people they had been seeing for a while. Pastor Mike's wife, Mary, introduced them to a few of the couples that were near their age. There was another couple they were introduced to that was expecting their first child as well. No dates were set but there was the start of possible friendships among them before they left to go home.

Chapter Eighteen

Homer was at his momma's grave site one afternoon after leaving Frank and Ron in charge of the service station. He studied the stone that they had placed on her grave and remembered some of the times that he had had as he was growing up. He was remembering the emptiness of their lives for so many years while in the shack. He was trying to decide if he should have left home earlier in life and if he had ever thought he could do something about the anger that surrounded the home. He could not remember one time when he wanted to leave his momma. He wondered if he had been around other people if the desire to change would have come sooner than it did. It was so different now with Alice by his side and he was going to be a father in a few months. How was he going to learn how to be a father? He was having all these thoughts when someone spoke to him from nearby. He turned to see Miss Brown standing nearby. He said, "Hello Miss Brown."

She answered, "Hello Homer, I haven't seen you in a while. How are things going for you?"

Homer smiled as he said, "It seems a lifetime ago that you helped me. This is my momma's grave that I am visiting. I now own the service station and have some men who work for me. I am now married, and I am going to be a father in a few months. I don't know if I ever thanked you for the help, you gave me when I needed it."

Miss Brown smiled back as she said, “You have been busy haven’t you. I am sorry to hear about your momma. Both of my parents are buried over here. I knew after I met you that your uncle was correct and that you were merely unlearned and not at all stupid. You made my work easy with your overwhelming desire to change your life. Congratulations on your marriage and upcoming child. How does all this make you feel?”

Homer seemed to contemplate his answer, “I came here today to think about how I feel. I spent my life so isolated that I have never been around children, and I do not know if I will be a good father. My wife Alice has been so understanding with my lack of ability around people and, so we usually talk it out and we create a plan on how Jesus would have us live. We have been talking lately about how her friends have stopped being around her since we married so we are trying to make new friends at the church we attend. I miss my momma not seeing some of the things happening in my life, but I have only been able to learn how to not do things from her. My coming to her grave encourages me to keep learning how to be around people and not go back to the loneliness.”

Miss Brown said, “I have never heard anyone speak so openly about how they feel and why they feel the way they do. Most people do not want to change, nor do they want to be told how to live. I find it very admirable that you and your wife can plan together for your lives. I am sure you will be a great father because you are so unsure of yourself that you will always monitor how you act. No one really knows how they will act as they become parents but most of them have had parents to show them at least one example of how to do it. You know what has harmed you more than what you know about being happy. You have determined to turn that into a positive influence in your life and you will bestow it on your family. It was nice seeing you Homer, and I hope I hear from you again. Goodbye!"

Homer watched as she turned and went back to her car and left. He stayed for a few more minutes and then went back to the garage to end the day. He was going to meet with a new teenager who wanted to work for him at the station. The young man was still in high school and would be for another year. When asked if he would be willing to work Saturdays, it came out that it would interfere with his high school sports, and he would not take the job.

Alice stopped by as she usually did after work and Homer could see that she was quite upset. He went into the office with her and asked her what the problem was. Alice said, "The directors of the library asked me if I was going to come back to work after having the baby. I told them that I intended to come back, but I was not sure if I would be able to. They then told me that they were going to take the decision into their own hands. They have hired a new librarian to take my place and she is going to start in two weeks. They are letting me go and hiring her."

By then, Alice was crying, and Homer tried to comfort her with a hug. He told her that she should go home for now and that things would be just as Jesus would have them to be. He told her that he would bring the deposit home like they did on weekends and just bring it back tomorrow. He told her he would be home as soon as he locked up for the night.

Homer did as he had promised Alice and took the books home with him tonight. He hurried with the animals and went in to be with his wife. He found her still crying and he said, “I don’t know what to say to you, but I am glad that you are going to be by my side more and you will be able to take care of our child without sending her to some program as a babysitter. We do not need the money as much as we once did so that is not a problem. Can you tell me why you are so upset at this?”

Alice answered, “I just was not ready to leave my job and know that I could not go back to it. They said that it was not because of my work but that it was hard to find qualified people when they needed them. This woman came by and spoke to them, and they decided it would be safer for them to hire her now than to have to look for someone if I could not return to work after having our baby. I was afraid of what you might think if I did not have a job to go back to.”

Homer gently instructed her, “I want you to be happy more than anything else. We do not need the money as much as I need your help with the bookkeeping and to be the mother of our child. I would be able to do more work in the shop myself if you could come for a few hours during the week. The animal meat is still growing in sales and that takes a few of my hours on Saturday as well. I hope you are not too disappointed at what they have done."

Alice sniffled as she said, "I just did not want to add any pressure to you. I have my pride to deal with, but I can deal with that. You are so special to me."

The conversation was interrupted by the knock on the door. It was Uncle Jake and a stranger that Homer did not know. His uncle asked if they could come in and they were offered a chair in the living room. Jake apologized for the late hour but said, "I had to come over here tonight and let you meet this young man. I just met him a couple of hours ago and we have been talking for that long. I had trouble believing the story that he was telling me, but he has me convinced that he was telling the truth. Homer, do you remember when you asked me if we had any other living relatives and I told you no?"

Homer's face showed anxiety, "I remember it was at the time momma introduced me to my pa's brother Stanley. I was so hurt with the loneliness that I was angry with momma for not letting me know we had kin. Is this man related to Uncle Stanley?"

Jake said, "Yes he is, and he is also related to you and to me."

Homer asked with some confusion, "How can that be? You had no children, and I was the only one living with momma. Are you going to make me mad at my momma after she is dead?"

Jake tried to evade the answer, "I am going to let this man tell you part of the story and his name is Jed like your grandpa and my dad."

Jed was extremely nervous as he began to tell his story again, "I was born twenty years ago in a mining town a few miles from here. I was raised by two loving parents with no other siblings. My father worked in the mines and my mother took up sewing as well as raising me. I had a normal childhood and went to school like the rest of the kids in town. The one thing that I know about other children and adults is that they can be mean when they want to be. I had my share of fights growing up with kids that wanted to prove something or other. The one thing that was usually thrown in my face is how I did not look like my parents. My father had red hair and my mother had auburn hair with blue eyes. She was a very pretty woman to look at, but she loved my father and I never saw her look at another man in my life. I did not go to work in the mines but stayed in the town where I grew up. My father died of black lung disease a couple of years ago and I moved into the house to help my mother finish paying the bank for it. She pined away for a while and then started to come out of it a little. We were talking one night, and I asked her why she never had any more children. I do not know if it was the pain of losing her husband or just a sense of guilt that made her tell me that she never had any children. I heard a story about how a recently widowed woman had given me to them to raise as their own. She had another child that was over two years old and did not have the money to raise him to say nothing about having another new baby. I was so angry that I left the house that night. I had to find out what parts of my life were real and what parts were lies. I finally went back a couple of months ago and my mother told me the name of the woman who had allowed them to raise me. She told me how they had wanted to tell me some day about my adoption but never had a reason to do it. She told me how she could never have children but had wanted an heir for her husband. That is why they accepted me as their son. I then needed to find out all that I could about a woman who had moved out of town almost twenty years ago."

Homer interrupted, "You went looking for my momma didn't you. How could she have done that to us? I suppose that you were the lucky one that did not have to live with her and her anger. Uncle Jake, didn't you know that I had a brother?"

Jake said, "Your momma did not come back to town until she lost the house where she had been living. She must have given birth sometime after your pa died and when she came back to live on the farm. She went to the grave with the knowledge of Jed's birth. I know that she was an incredibly angry person from the time she came home but she never let anyone know the source of all her anger."

Alice could feel Homer shaking as she held his hand in hers. The room went silent for a few minutes and then Homer said, "Why did you come and what do you expect now you have found out some of this?"

Jed said, "I just heard you speak about the anger your mother had as you were growing up. I became angry about how I was raised with my mother, but I really did not mean to hurt her with my search for my real mother. I guess I did not care if I hurt her some in my anger, but I will go back and make that right with her. I would like to know how life could have been and to meet you now that I know you exist. I never in my life thought that I was brother to someone I did not know. I guess that Jake is my uncle also, but he did not want to tell me anything until we met. Do you think that you could share some of the things that I could know about my real mother and yourself someday soon?"

Homer slowly said, "I believe that we could do that someday and I am not really surprised to find out what my momma did. I will just tell you this tonight, you were better off with your adoptive momma than with your real one. No wonder she would never speak about her life before and would not go back to the old town. She passed away several months ago from a severe stroke and I could take you to see the grave in the future as well."

There was little conversation from that point on. Jed asked if he could come back the next Sunday afternoon and visit the grave with them. It was agreed upon and Jed left for home. Jake looked at Homer and said, "I guess that Sis did what she thought was right, but she never said anything about Jed to me. We did not see each other on a regular basis, and she could have been pregnant when your pa died, and we would not have known about it. We both saw what she did when she had to leave the cabin, so his story is very believable. I was shocked to find out who he was when he came to the door and spoke with your aunt and me. I do not think that our parents knew what she did before they died, or they would have been angry with her for that. I will stop by and see you one night this week and we can talk about it some more. Good night."

Homer never said another word that night as he went in and joined Alice and the baby in their bed. Alice knew better than to start a conversation and just kissed him as they went to sleep.

Homer and Alice went to church in the morning and asked Pastor Mike if he would meet with them as soon as possible after work this week. They agreed on Tuesday night at the church and then they left without their usual fellowship after the service. They went for a walk later in the afternoon and Homer stopped at the site of the old shack. He made his first comment about the visit as he stared at the ashes. He said, "I wonder why she didn't give me away also?"

Pastor Murray greeted them at the door to his office on Tuesday after work. They made some small talk before Pastor Mike asked them what the problem was.

Homer started, "We had a visitor the other night. It was a young man that I had never met. He told us a story that I find very believable and now I am not sure how to act. He told us how my momma had given him to another family to raise after he had been born. We have no reason not to believe him, and all the parts fit with what we know did happen. My momma went to her grave and never spoke of him again."

Pastor Mike said, "Wow! That is news to receive out of the blue. You say that she never told anyone about this supposed brother that came to your door."

Homer said, "As far as we know, she never told her parents or anyone else up to the day that she died. His name is Jed and he is named after my grandfather. He wanted to know what his life would have been like if she had not given him away. I only told him that it sounded like he had a better life with his adoptive parents. He is coming back this Sunday to visit her grave with us and maybe talk some more."

Pastor Mike said, "I will tell you something that you may not want to hear but I did not know what it meant at the time. I went to visit someone else in the care home one day and I saw your momma there as well. She had a pad of paper and scribbled out what I now believe to have been the name Jed and she was crying at the time. I tried to understand what she was trying to say but she had to be calmed down by the nurses in her desperate attempt to tell me whatever she wanted to say. She passed before I ever got back to see her again. She may have been trying to tell me about Jed at that time. I would like to know how I can help you now. I imagine it brought out some of the old anger at your mother to find this out."

Homer answered, "How could she have been willing to hurt so many people in the ways that she did? I find myself wondering why she did not give me away also, so she could have been totally alone. I know that she kept me lonely and when the time came, I was ready to change but I never wanted to hurt her. Uncle Jake says they call it depression for the condition that my momma had but I am starting to believe that she wanted other people to hurt as much as she did. I do not want to be angry with her and I certainly do not blame Jed for what has happened. I just don't understand all the hurt that she was willing to cause."

Pastor Mike tried to comfort him as he said, "She did hurt a lot of people in her life, and I believe that she hurt you the most after herself. You can let the hurt destroy your life the way that she destroyed her own or you can let Jesus heal you with His forgiveness toward your momma. You have a totally new life now. You have a loving wife and soon will have a child of your own. You have a business of your own and people who work for you. You learned to read and write so you could change but your momma could never find forgiveness for herself and change the way she lived. The internal pressure brought on a stroke and that finally ended her physical suffering, but it was in a state of unforgiveness with her own actions. She allowed her soul to be tormented for what she had done but it never took the place of coming to Jesus for forgiveness for the things she had done. Jesus is the one who showed us how to forgive those who hurt us and to live in peace with them. You may go to Jesus to forgive her actions toward you and your brother Jed, or you will become as bitter as she was. You chose the better way, and you can choose it again. Do you understand what I mean?"

Homer was teary as he said, "I believe that I do. I had to choose to change when I went to work for my uncle and left her to be alone. Once I turned away from the loneliness that she had kept me in, I was able to live by making decisions on my own. My wife has taught me how to love in ways that I never understood while with my momma. I believe that she was looking to change when she had her first stroke, but it was too late. I do not have time to be angry with her now any more than I could back then. There is a wonderful freedom to be found in forgiving someone enough to not let them control you by keeping you angry. I had to do that once and I can share that forgiveness with my brother Jed if he needs help in forgiving momma."

Pastor Mike seemed pleased as he said, "That would be a wonderful thing if you helped him not be mad at your momma, but he will have to forgive her himself to find the freedom that you speak of. Let me know if you need some help from me in the future. Let Alice help you if you start to feel anger and let her love for you be a guide to a deeper lasting freedom. Let me say a prayer before we go our separate ways."

Homer's Shack

Chapter Nineteen

Homer was sitting in their living room with his Uncle Jake and Aunt Flora. They had shared a piece of cake and coffee and were starting to talk about Jed. Homer said, "We had a nice talk with Pastor Mike Tuesday after work and he encouraged me in not becoming bitter at my momma. He thinks the word that she wrote for him when he visited her might have been the name Jed. She could not express herself anymore and became frustrated at not being able to finish what she was trying to say. I just wonder if she ever would have told me about Jed."

Flora said, "The one thing that I don't understand is the fact that she already knew that I could not have children with your uncle, but she never came to us for help. We would have been glad to raise him until she could get better."

Jake said, "Now Flora, I don't want you to start picking up any bitterness at Sis for some of the decisions that she made. Our lives have been blessed in other ways than having children and we have been able to work with Homer and help him tremendously. The Lord Jesus knows what is best for us if we trust him and He did not want us to raise children of our own. It sounded to me as if Jed had a reasonably good life with his adoptive parents. Besides, we cannot change what Sis did now and we will probably have to guess why she did it the way she did. We need to believe that Jesus wanted to bless that other couple with a child for a few years. Times were hard for the miners during those years trying to raise a family and working in the mines. Those years of hard work killed Jed's adoptive father and Sis's anger killed her while they were both still young. How do you feel about this Homer?"

Homer had been listening to his aunt and uncle but answered, "I do not want to guess why she did what she did. I do not blame Jed in any way, and it is quite easy to understand what my momma did. I want to meet him and see if our lives are meant to join in any meaningful way now. It is not like he needs to make a choice about where he wants to live; it is a decision about how we all want to live now we know. I could be mad at him for having a better life with his parents than having lived with my momma, but I agree with you Uncle Jake that Jesus knows what is best for us. If I died suddenly and Alice was not able to care for our baby, she might have to do the same thing as my momma did. The facts are that she would be able to care for our child if I should die but I intend to be here to see him or her grow up. None of us were there when she made her decision, so we must trust that Jesus made it as good as possible."

Alice reached over and held his hand and said, "You better stay here and help me raise our child. I have not met our child yet, but I know that I want to share its life and I believe that Sis had to do what she did. I only wish that she could have forgiven herself after a while and gotten a little peace in her life. Anger is such a negative thing to have in your life."

Homer added to her comments as he said, “I hope that Jed has not hurt his adoptive momma with all this, or my momma’s anger will win again. Why don’t we plan on all having dinner together after we go to the grave site? We can all get a chance to hear the same thing at the same time and we can tell him how we feel and why. He left without telling us how we could get a hold of him, or I would ask him to bring his adoptive momma with him. I hate to break up a swell party, but I need to go to work early, and I know that Alice is tired, so we will all say good night for now.”

Frank had brought one of the young men that he knew in town and had him come to see about working for Homer. Frank introduced Glen Hopkins to Homer and then went to work. Homer asked him to tell a few things about why he wanted to work.

Glen said, “Everyone must work eventually, and I could help my family if I was working. I am the oldest of four children and we live near Frank. We go to the same school, but he is two years older than me. I am willing to work a lot of hours and I do not have anything that would keep me from working on Saturday like the other guy who came to ask for work. I know that you could teach me, and I will not forget what you taught me. Please give me a try and you won’t be sorry.”

Homer said, “I will give you a chance. I will need to have Frank and I will train you, so you can do credit cards and how to be polite to the customers. I will warn Frank also that if I hear that you two are talking and not taking care of my customers, it will not go well with you two. Now you two get together and tell me what your schedule is like, so I can work with you together until I feel you are trained. Welcome to the group Glen."

Sunday afternoon found several people standing over a recent grave site on a sunny day. Jed was told that they would like him to come to the farm again for the meal and to talk some more. He was hesitant at first but then decided he could stay for a while. They went and sat on Homer's back porch and were having some ice-cold sun tea.

Jed started, "You have a nice place here. Was this where you grew up?"

Jake piped in, "This was my father Jed's farm where Sis and I grew up. Sis moved out of town when she married Homer's father and I presume yours also. I took over the farm when our parents died. I moved into the main house from the house that Homer lives in here. I tried to have Sis move in here years ago, but she called it charity and chose to live in a tar paper shack near the end of the farm. It had no electricity and no bathroom, and everything was done on a wood cook stove. I had to move her into the house when the town condemned it because of not having a toilet. Sis had the last say about the matter when she burned the shack down herself. That was over a year ago now."

Jed asked, "Homer, you were raised in that shack?"

Homer hesitated and then began, "The shack is all I can

remember of growing up. I never really went to school, so it was just my momma and I for many years. I worked for the neighbors some for money and I would snare rabbits and other wild game for meat. Uncle Jake would take my momma to town every so often and she would buy what we needed such as flour, lard, and seeds. Momma was an incredibly angry person her entire life. We were just starting to speak about her feelings when she had her first stroke. Even when she spoke of losing pa, she never spoke about you. Did you tell your adoptive mother that you had found us?"

Jed said, "I went to see her the next day and we had an exceedingly long talk. She said it was not unusual for a family to raise someone else's child back then. They only had to make my name change in the records for it to be legal. She spoke of your momma being beside herself in grief and that she would just mope around the house the few times that she went back to see her. She said that she offered to take you in also when she would find you crying and hungry in your crib, but she wanted to keep you. A few months after I went with them, your mother disappeared without a trace, and I do not think they ever saw each other again. My mother says that she is sorry that she could not keep us together."

Homer hesitated before he said, "I want to be angry for momma giving you away, but I can't do it. It sounds to me like the parents who raised you loved you very much. I learned to read and write after going to work for Uncle Jake so that I could change the way we lived. Even then, I could not do it because I was angry but because I loved her. I can honestly say that I have let go of the anger that I did have and only want to live the best we can from now on. I don't know if you are looking to become part of our lives or if you just can go home and be at peace now."

Jed said, "I know that I can go home and be at peace now. I do not know how much our lives will join but it looks as if I am going to become an uncle myself and I was not sure that was ever going to happen. When is the baby due Alice?"

Alice answered, "In just a couple more months. This is my last week of work at the library, and they have hired someone to replace me permanently."

Jake piped in, "In your search, did you know that your father had a brother. You have Uncle Stanley, and he lives near you with his family. I still can't believe that no one knew about you for all these years."

They were interrupted by Aunt Flora declaring that the meal was ready, and they should come and get a plate before it got cold. They finished the meal and Jed thanked them but said he had to get home to go to work in the morning at the newspaper. This time they exchanged telephone numbers before everyone left.

Homer had a lot of help in the garage over the next two weeks. Glen turned out to be very friendly even though he was very shy. When he was face to face with people, he could do everything that the job demanded and more. Frank started to just watch him after a few days unless there was more than one car in the yard. Frank was also at the point where he could change tires and do the kind of work that Homer had started out doing with his uncle. Alice would come to the station a couple of days per week and do her shopping so Homer would not have to do it after work. At the end of the two weeks, the service station was becoming a well-oiled machine of people.

The selling of animal meat was becoming more of a distraction than a monetarily stabilizing factor in the whole of their lives. Homer decided that he would sell the rabbits and the pens if he could. The chickens were not as much a bother as they cared for themselves if you kept water and feed available to them when they wanted it. They also found a shop where they would kill and pluck the chickens for them and give them back frozen and ready for their freezer. Jake and he figured that they would start smaller flocks of chickens, so they would have room for the meat at the time of slaughter if they had them all butchered at once.

Jake and Flora went on another trip earlier than they had planned so they could be home near the time of the baby's delivery. Between Flora, Mrs. Moodie and her sister, Alice was going to have someone with her during the day until she delivered. Homer was at the point that he got nervous every time Alice called him on the phone because she was still alone for another week or so. The boys at the service station started to pick on him about how nervous he was getting but they all could laugh about it.

Jed called a couple of times over the two-week period and Homer asked him to bring his adoptive mother out, so he could meet her. Jed asked her if she wanted to do that, and a date was set for them to meet again.

Homer and Alice met with Jed and his mother Faith Young on a Saturday after delivering the meat. They met at a diner instead of them driving all the way to meet each other. Alice sat in a chair instead of booth for her comfort at the end of their booth. Jed introduced his mother as he sat down across from Homer. They made some small talk as they ordered some coffee from the waitress named Dee.

Homer started, "I would like to thank you for caring for Jed the way that you did for all those years."

Tears started to well up in Faith's eyes as she looked at Homer. She said, "I don't know how you can say that. I know that you are sincere, but we only saw a need and knew that we could help. My husband Cecil worked at the mines with your father before he died. Your father was telling everyone at the mines how your mother was expecting their second child. We happened to stop by to see how she was doing after your father passed and we found her in a terrible state of mind. Jed was just born, and she could not bring, herself to nurse him and he was very hungry. We went out and got some bottles and some milk and came back to feed the baby. As we were leaving after feeding Jed, she told us to take him and raise him because she could not do it. That is what we did. I went back a couple of times to check on you, but she would not let us take you with us. Then she just disappeared from town. We never told Jed that he was not our own child until Cecil passed on. I am sorry for the hurt that keeping such a secret has caused him." She stopped after making that comment and looked at Jed who returned the look.

Homer added, "I am not mad that you could not keep us together, but I spent years of loneliness with a terribly angry woman. She took most of that anger to her grave. The hard times in our lives can make us stronger or they can destroy someone like it did for my momma. You were a blessing to Jed sent by Jesus, and He will thank you for that someday."

By this time, the tears were streaming freely down her cheeks. She could not speak but Jed said, "I told you that you would not have to worry about meeting my brother. I do not think he has a mean bone in his body. I love you mother and I am not angry with you either. I just had to know more of the truth about how things were when I was born. I feel that I would be dead now if you had not come along and maybe Homer also."

They continued to speak for twenty more minutes about Alice's due date and things at work. The goodbyes were lingering as they separated and went home in different directions. A different kind of family was forming as they spent time together and they all knew it. Homer made the parting comment that she would find a different scenario if she came to visit this newborn at his home and

Faith said she agreed.

Mr. and Mrs. Moodie stayed to share the meal that she had prepared as she stayed with Alice during the day. Mrs. Moodie asked Homer, "How does it feel to have a new twenty-year-old brother? Alice says that he seems genuinely nice and wants to get to know all of you better."

Homer eagerly said, "You can only imagine the surprise given to us when he came to our door with my uncle. Jed did not have to give his entire story before I knew where it was going to end up. I am only glad that it has a happy ending, and he did not die at my momma's hand. Mr. and Mrs. Young raised him as if he were their own and they loved him as a baby and still do. More people should be able to show their love the way that they did and help someone in dire need."

Mr. Moodie commented, "Not many people have a happy ending with the problems in their lives. Life loves to keep giving you troubles to face until you die if you let it. We will help you clean up the table and things and we will be going home so you can all rest for tomorrow. I believe that your aunt is going to be around tomorrow to stay with Alice. By the way, do you two have names for the baby yet?"

Alice said, "We are still trying to narrow down the field of names for a girl, but a boy will be called Robert. We both want the first child to be a boy anyway, so we haven't decided on a girl's name yet."

Mr. Moodie chuckled as he said, "Give him a middle name that starts with an O and his initials can be his nickname."

Everyone chuckled at the idea, but Alice said they would give it some thought. The evening was quickly succumbed to sleep once her parents left for the night.

Homer had just gotten back from a trip to the bank when he got a phone call from his aunt. She asked him to come home, so he could take Alice to the hospital because it was time. Homer went into overdrive as he raced out the door and told the guys that he might not be back today and that they should lock up when they left. He hurried home and parked the car right beside the steps to the house. He ran in and heard Alice moaning with the onset of another contraction. He was about to panic when his aunt told him that everything was going well, and it was all normal. His aunt told him that she had called the doctor and they were expecting them in a little while. As the contraction subsided, Alice could walk out to the car with little trouble. They put the suitcase in the back seat that they had prepared for her stay at the hospital and then they were off. His aunt told him that the first deliveries always took a little longer and there was no reason to drive in an unsafe manner. Alice asked Aunt Flora to call her mother as they were going down the driveway.

Homer drove in a determined fashion as they went to the

hospital. Alice had a few more contractions during the trip and each one made him more nervous about what was happening. They arrived at the hospital and Alice was seated in a wheelchair and taken to the labor room. Homer was left in the waiting room to give the information to a receptionist. When that was done, he was offered a seat, but he asked when he would be allowed to see Alice. The receptionist told him that the doctor would be out to speak to him when he had a chance. Those were not the words that Homer wanted to hear, and he tried to insist on going to see her. The receptionist told him that it was not possible because of all the things that had to be done before the baby was born. Homer conceded to her wishes but in a very reluctant way.

The waiting room was not all that conducive for a restful wait. Homer would sit for a while and then get up and pace for a while. The first time that he really noticed the clock it read three-thirty. He had been there a while when Mrs. Moodie showed up. Homer told him how they were not letting him see Alice up to this point. Mrs. Moodie did explain some of the things that had to be done so that Alice could deliver. That explained some things to Homer, but it did not make him any less irritated with not being able to be with Alice. They had been there almost an hour when the doctor finally came out to speak to Homer.

The doctor explained, "Everything is going fine, but she has not dilated very much yet and that means it will be a while before the baby is born. I can let you go up to the labor room where she is now but only for a short time, and you will have to come back here and wait. Do you want to do that now?"

They followed the doctor through a series of halls and then into a room near the maternity ward. They had to put on some gowns and masks and then he took them in to see Alice. She was on a table in the middle of the room and her lower body was draped with blankets, so they could not see. She looked up at them as Homer bent over to give her a kiss. He took her by the hand and rubbed it as he asked her how she felt. Alice said, "This is the part that every mother has concerns about, but it must happen for the child to come and live with us. I will be all right and so will the baby. I love you and I will see you in a little while."

Homer replied how he loved her also and then they were escorted back to the waiting room. They had not been back long when several other family members arrived to join in the wait. Uncle Jake and Aunt Flora went out in another hour and got everyone some sandwiches from a little café down the street. Homer was doing his best to stay calm, but he would turn to look at every person who walked past the door. It was a little after eight at night when the doctor came back to the room. He shook Homer's hand and congratulated him on having a newborn son. The rest of the family was told that Homer would be the only one allowed to see her tonight because of the lateness of the delivery but they could come during visiting hours the next day. Alice was tired but everything about the birth had been normal, and the baby was doing very well. The family all congratulated Homer as he was being taken to see Alice and his son Robert for the first time and they said they would see him tomorrow.

Homer entered the room and found Alice resting on the bed and watching a crib through a window. He said, "Hello momma. How are you feeling now that it is over?"

Alice said, "I would not want to do that every day, but I got to hold Robert for a few seconds before they took him in to clean him and weigh him. He has a good cry, so I will be able to hear him in the night. Can you see him in that crib in there?"

Homer walked over to the glass, so he could get a better look at the tiny human being lying there. There was some dark hair sticking out of the blue bonnet that they had on his head, and he was moving his arms a little in his sleep. Homer told Alice how proud he was of her and said he would be back in the morning as early as he could. Homer said, "I was thinking of what your father said and what would you think of the middle name being Oswald, so his initial would spell Rob. He would be named Robert Oswald Baker."

Alice smiled as she said, "That would be fine, and it will please my father that we did as he suggested. I think I will go to sleep now. I'll see you tomorrow."

Chapter Twenty

Homer went to the garage in the morning but mostly to tend to the deposits before going to see Alice and Robert. The guys working at the station were glad to hear that everything had gone well, and both were healthy. Homer also had to make a stop today at the appliance store. He was going to have an automatic clothes washer and dryer put in the house while Alice was still in the hospital and surprise her when she got home. The job of washing baby diapers sounded tedious if not difficult and the new machines would simplify the task. Alice had not asked for them, but he wanted life to remain as pain free as possible. He had spoken to the owner of the store in advance, and he only had to go by and tell them to bring them out at noon, so he could let them in. They were going to be installed in the kitchen for now, so Alice did not have to do stairs with the baby.

Homer arrived at the hospital and found Alice still nursing the baby. She said, "Robert was a little slow waking up and getting started this morning, so we are not done yet. You can hold him for a few minutes when he gets done before they take him back for a nap. He certainly has a good appetite."

Homer stood smiling as he watched the two of them. He said, "You seem to take to the job of being a mother pretty well for a beginner."

They both chuckled at his comment. Alice took the baby

and wiped his mouth before handing him to Homer. She said, "Just place your hand behind his neck and support him because he is not strong enough to do that yet. You can cradle him in your arms, or you can lay him against your chest. You can even sit in that chair over there with him and rock him."

Homer had only been there a few minutes when a nurse knocked on the door to take Robert back to the nursery. They told Homer that he could have him back tonight when he came back. There was another knock on the door, and it was Alice's mother. She poked her head in and said that she could come back later but Homer assured her that he had to go back to the station for a couple more hours before he could come back. Homer kissed Alice as he left, and Mrs. Moodie remained for a little while.

Frank and Glen had the duty on Saturday. Homer delivered the meat and stopped to pick up the deposit as the service station was going to stay open until six o'clock today and from now on. Homer had to hurry things as Alice and Robert were coming home today. Friends and neighbors had supplied the nursery with all the supplies they would need to begin with. The Moodies had brought a crib and baby changer they had in their garage. Some of the women in the church had given her a baby basket with diapers, powders, diaper pins, crib blankets, and some baby outfits. Jake and Flora gave them two dozen diapers and some rubber pants. With the addition of the washer and dryer, Alice should be ready to bring Robert home.

Homer went up to the room and told Alice and the nurses that he was there, and they were ready to go home. The nurses did the final paperwork and the three of them were ready to go. Homer brought the car up to the door of the hospital and Alice got into the front seat with him. The nurse gave the baby to Alice and wished them well as she turned and went back inside.

Homer's pride was showing as he said, "I have been working on getting the house ready for the two of you. You know the crib is in our room for now, but I put the changing table in the corner of the living room by moving one of the chairs. I did a couple of other things that you will be able to see when you get there but I am so glad that you are coming home. I won't have some nurse taking Robert out of my arms while I am at home."

Alice giggled at his last comment. She said, "In about a year, you will be wishing someone would take him out of your arms, so you can have a minute of peace and quiet. I am glad to be coming home and getting into my own bed to rest. I think the hospital mattresses are filled with beans or something else that is lumpy. If I had more time, I would go down there and teach someone how to cook food without overdoing it. I shouldn't complain because my stay was comfortable for the most part."

They were pulling up to the house and there were several familiar cars in the driveway. All the Moodie's were there, and Jake and Flora were keeping them entertained as they waited for them to arrive home. This was going to be the first time that her father and sister had gotten to hold the baby. It would also be the first time that Jake and Flora even saw them since Alice was taken to the hospital. Homer pulled up by the porch and opened the door for Alice. He took Robert from her arms as she got out of the car and then gave him back to her as they walked in. They opened the door, and a loud cheer went up for them as the mob formed around them.

Alice said, "Please give me room to breathe. We are going to be home for a long time, and you can all have a turn if you want it but give us a chance to come in the door and put down the extra stuff from the hospital."

With those words spoken, a path cleared for them to the living room. Alice took a minute to assess the changes to the house that Homer had made while she was gone. She said that the changing table should work there and the crib in the bedroom was her idea anyway. Then she saw something white in the kitchen that she did not recognize. She yelled, "Homer, what have you done to my kitchen? Are those what I think they are?" She turned and looked at Homer with tears in her eyes. Then she handed the baby to her sister and gave Homer a big hug and kiss for the new washer and dryer.

The family all took turns holding the baby as Alice rested in her chair in the living room. They had been there for a little over an hour and Robert started to fuss while being held by Mr. Moodie. Alice told them that he was probably hungry and asked if they could leave them, so they could get settled in now that they were home. They all got their belongings and left right away. Alice went into her room and changed into some clothing that would make it easier to feed Robert from. She then took her seat back and Homer handed her the baby. He asked her if she would be okay when he went out to tend to the animals and then he would come in and make them something to eat. He returned quickly from the barns and looked in the refrigerator for what he could find there. Alice said she had never seen him make anything, but a bread sandwich and Homer put on a pouty face at her. Homer simply told her that he did not want her to know that he could cook so she would not ask him to do it on a regular basis.

Homer awoke in the darkness and realized that he had heard the baby give a little whimper. He then sensed that Alice got out of bed and started to feed him again as he fell back to sleep. It was still dark when the baby let out another whimper and Alice fed him again. It did not take him long to realize that their sleep pattern was going to be changed from now on. They chose not to go to church this week, so Alice could get in a couple of short naps between feedings and diaper changes. They were surprised to hear a knock on the door early in the afternoon. Homer went to the door and found Pastor Mike and his wife Mary standing at the door. Homer welcomed them in and announced them to Alice as they entered the living room. They gave Alice a set of lotions for the baby and congratulated them both.

Mary asked the new mother, "Have you gotten tired enough to be able to fall asleep in the daytime yet? It is something that most of us must learn in the beginning of child raising."

Alice answered, "It is not as much a problem of falling asleep as it is a concern of not hearing the baby if I am asleep. I probably should not worry because he has a good cry when he wants to. I think Homer heard us every time last night."

Homer nodded his head as he said, "I went right back to sleep and thought that maybe I should feel guilty, but I don't have what it takes to feed him."

They all chuckled at him as they just spent some time in fellowship before Pastor Mike prayed over Robert and his parents as they were leaving. Homer and Alice received the blessing of their house and their child from the pastor they had come to love and respect.

The service station now had to measure the gasoline in their tanks daily and call in to the supplier if they got below a certain point to prompt a delivery. Frank and Glen were keeping the station open to six o'clock for six days per week as well as the mechanical work they were doing. Glen was true to his word about not having to be shown twice how to do things and he was becoming a good mechanic in his own timing. Homer bought each of the young men a base cabinet to start buying their own tools for their future. The service station owned an entire line of pneumatic tools now for all the men to share. Homer even offered to pay the tuition for the young men as they took classes on the new electronics being installed into automobiles. It seemed to be a quickly changing world and Homer wanted to stay with the times to not be pushed out of the business. Ron, who was getting on in years, asked to be allowed to remain uneducated about the electronics and he would allow the youngsters to do that work.

Jed had been told the fact that he was now an uncle and he asked to come by on Sunday afternoon that week. Homer and Alice were glad to see him arrive that Sunday and he had brought Faith Young with him. They each had a package in their hands as they walked into the house. Jed walked over to his nephew and had a look at the newborn. He was joined by Faith and then they went to the living room. Jed presented them with a gift certificate, so they could have pictures taken of the baby at a shop nearby.

Faith said, “Jed does not know what I brought today. I have kept it a secret for twenty years and I thought it was a good time to bring it out for him to see. This package has the outfit that he was in when we brought him home from his mother’s house and it also has the hospital bracelet that has his name on it before we had it changed. I would like to give you the clothing and to give Jed the bracelet now.”

The outfit was simply a newborn’s suit in blue with some animals in darker blue throughout. Homer thanked her for it but asked Jed if he wanted to keep it. Jed said, “I want Robert to have it after all these years. I would like to keep the bracelet in memory of the years that followed that day. It represents my two fathers and my two lives. It tells of one father that I never met before his death and the one that taught me how to live right up to his own death. I had a chance to mourn for one and the love he had given me and the love of the one who created me who is represented in Homer is now a pleasant memory. The troubling of my mind is over now that I know the entire truth of how it came to be."

Jed and Faith both got a chance to hold Robert before they left to go home again. Faith spoke of his looks very much like Jed did as a baby and told them she would look for a photo to bring the next time.

Homer and Alice were speaking to the man with whom they had done their investing. They wanted to add some more money to their account and ask if they should add Robert's name on the account. They were told that all their investments were doing well but Texas Instruments was doing the best of all. It had changed in price to one dollar per share in just over a year and the representative told them that it was a four-hundred percent increase. He did tell them that they did not have to add Robert's name because of his direct kinship to them. They were told that if they ever created a living trust that it would be time to place his name on the papers. They put the entire amount that they wanted to add to the portfolio in Texas Instruments and then left for home satisfied.

Homer and Alice were speaking on the way home from the man's office about what they owed and to whom. Homer said, "The service station is still paying for some of the tools that I have bought but they will be paid off in two months or less. The parts store has been great in helping us keep up with the times so far. The business loan that I took out to buy the service station is the only big item that we owe on."

Alice did say, "We still owe around half of the total bill at the hospital, but we could pay that today if we wanted to. You have been a great provider for us, and I am proud of you."

Homer said, "I feel as if I could pay the guys at the service station more and make them feel appreciated by us. I thought about making some jobs pay a bonus, but they work so well together that I do not want to interrupt that. I think that they all deserve more. I am thinking of selling the rabbits and their pens, so I could have more time on Saturdays."

Alice questioned him, "Are you sure you want to do that? You worked hard to get that business going and it is doing well for you currently. Is it the slaughtering that is bothering you or the commitment?"

Homer answered, "I am not sure that the time commitment is having significant rewards anymore. The only time that I can get away with you is after church on Sunday unless you all come with me on a Saturday."

Alice suggested, "I don't believe that you can only get away on Sunday. You have men that could take care of the business any day that you are gone. If we want to take a longer vacation, we could arrange it easily with your uncle or hire one of the guys for a period. What do you really want to do?"

Homer answered, "I want to be sure that I am not neglecting you and Rob during this time. You seem easy to please all the time, so I do not know if you are contented with the way things are."

Alice smiled as she said, "You have given me everything that I ever asked for and you have gotten me lots of things that I did not ask for such as the washer and dryer you had put in. I need to be careful what I say around you, or you will change it for me. I am glad that I never mentioned the moonlight keeping me awake at night or you would have moved the moon for me."

They both chuckled over that comment, and they continued home in a less serious mood. Homer just added, "I think I would have gotten you darker curtains first."

Frank and Glen came into the office the next Friday afternoon to see Homer. Frank said, "I think you made a mistake on our hours for last week."

Homer asked, "Did your pay stub say a different number of hours than you put in for?"

Frank looked at the stub again and then let out a holler. He said, "No, but the amount per hour has changed. If this is no mistake, thank you very much."

Homer said, "It is no mistake. All three of you work hard for me and I do appreciate it. I do not want to make a bonus system because of how well you work together so I made it all even. I had already told Ron that it was happening but asked him not to tell you two, so I could thank you for the good work that you are doing. Speaking of working, do you see that gas customer sitting out there?"

Alice laughed as Homer told her of the two men coming in with their pay checks to correct them. Alice said, "Too bad you didn't think to tell them that they had to pay it back and see the looks on their faces. I should know better than to think that you could be mean for even one minute. I love you!"

Chapter Twenty-One

Homer was trying to decide what he was going to buy his wife for her birthday in a couple of weeks. He wanted to make it something that she did not need for a change. He always purchased what they needed in a timely way, but he wanted this to be different. He had even asked his uncle what women might like and not ask for. His uncle had told him that jewelry usually fits into that category. He had decided to look in the jewelry store that was by the bank he was in at the time and find her a gift. The counter person asked if she could help Homer find anything special. Homer explained his desire to find Alice something for her birthday and then looked at some items she wanted to sell. Homer had already decided that he was not going to make it diamonds now and he walked over to a display of necklaces. The center piece was a beautiful silver chain necklace with a large turquoise pendant hanging between two linked smaller pendants similar in shape and color. Homer became fascinated with the piece. The clerk told him that she had matching earrings with the turquoise as well. The ensemble was a thing of beauty and elegance just begging to be worn by a blue-eyed woman such as Alice. The three items were placed in a gift box for Homer as he bought them.

Homer had also taken Alice's old car and gotten a new one with enough room for the baby and traveling needs such as a diaper bag and the like. He kept an older car that he did not mind getting grease and things on due to his work. He could not take the time to change clothing to go to the bank or similar places while at the service station.

Homer was at the station one day doing the deposit when a man parked near the door and came in to see Homer. The man was in an exquisite suit that was not often seen in this area. He got out of his car and just stood outside looking at the building and things across the street. He finally came in and asked for the owner. Homer introduced himself and asked what he could do for the man.

The man said, "I am Fred Little, and I work for the gasoline company that you sell for. I go around investigating our service stations and finding out what is working well for them and what we could do to help them. Your name was brought to my attention because of the increase in sales that you have had recently. You do not seem to have anything out of the ordinary such as a circus in your backyard to draw more people. You only have two gas pumps, so they must be terribly busy most of the time. I noticed two other service stations in town as I looked around before stopping and you are not in a major artery of traffic. How would you explain the reason for your success with our company?"

Homer simply stated, "Do you mean besides the blessing of Jesus? He is the reason we are doing well."

Mr. Little said, "I know of men who have made similar statements about the blessings of Jesus making things better but that does not create a good marketing statement for our shareholders. What do you think you are doing that draws your customers to your pumps?"

Homer said, "I am the third generation of my family to own this station. My grandfather built it and started it more than twenty years ago. My Uncle Jake ran it for years after my grandfather died and then he sold it to me. Your company put in the new pumps and fixed the outside of the station for me right after I bought it. They put in the pumps during the week that I was on my honeymoon. I made improvements to the inside myself. I was one of the first to take credit cards in the area and the first station with a canopy that you could light up at night. We are now open twelve hours per day for six days a week selling gas and doing car repairs. I have an older mechanic that is telling me that he is getting too old to do this much longer and two young men who help me. I am letting them take classes as well as supplying them with the best equipment we can have to do our work. We all work well together, and I am already looking for one more young man to have work for us. The only statement that I can think of is the fact that we care about our customers and treat them as we would like to be treated. My men know that they better be greeting customers with a smile, but they do it because they want to. I don't know if that tells you what you want to know or not."

Mr. Little continued as he looked around, "That is quite a story to be proud of. May I ask if you own the land on this side of the office?"

Homer pointed to a fence nearby and said, "I own beyond the fence, but I put the fence on my property to discourage people from pestering my good neighbors on that side. Why do you ask?"

Mr. Little said, "I am here for two reasons. Let me deal with the first one and then we will go back to reason number two." He went to his car and came out with a plaque that named Homer's service station as the most improved performance in gas sales in the entire state for the year. "This is a small token of our appreciation for what you have accomplished in the last year. In a couple of months, you will receive an invitation with tickets for a trip to our headquarters where you will be given the honors at a ceremony there. We will pay for the trip and the motel as well as meals for your coming to join us. We certainly hope that you can come."

Homer indignantly said, "Thank you for the plaque and we will have to see if my wife wants to make a trip with our new infant son or not at that time."

Mr. Little said, "Yes, we can discuss that again. Now, let us discuss number two of the reasons that I came today. Our company engineer still has the plans for your station and we have a proposal for you again. I would like to show you some plans for some possible improvements to your station. It would include removing this entire area where your office is and making a new wing against the service bays. We would create a new utility room, office, men's and lady's bathrooms, and an area big enough to sell convenient foods. This area here would have coolers for soft drinks or other cold drinks to be stored in. You could have a coffee island and you could have racks for chips and other similar walk out foods. There would be an area for a cashier and a cash register by the door. You would have entire control over what products you would sell in your store along with our products you carry now. We are willing to take, and have you shadow along with the owners of a similar store for a couple of days to see if it is anything you would like to do before you decide. You would be responsible for the inventory of your store, and we would not supply anything that was not our products. We are offering this to you as one of our proven future oriented owners. We would do all the remodeling for you with as little interruption with your current business as possible. We have crews of men who are familiar with all aspects of what you need, and they get it done quickly. You will be amazed at how much more you can earn with this kind of improvement to your building. We would also offer to bring in some new style pumps where you could fill four cars where you are filling two now. You would still own the building once we had done the improvements and it would be yours to sell or leave to your children when the time arrives."

Homer commented, "That certainly would change things around here. Would there be some new requirements from your company you have not mentioned yet? I was never open on

Saturday before and I now see the benefit of being open on Saturday but that was a requirement the last time."

Mr. Little said, "We are suggesting that our service stations are open from five in the morning to eleven at night as soon as possible after the new store is functional. Would that be something that you could consider?"

Homer looked at the man, "I would have to speak to my wife about this and I would like to at least go see a similar store and how many people it takes to be open that many hours per week. I am not afraid of change and improving things and being first in your area is always a good thing as well. Why don't you contact me in a couple of days or however you want to do this?"

Homer, Alice, Jake, and Flora were having coffee in the living room after dinner. Homer had asked his uncle to come over and see if he had some advice for the situation. Homer was holding Rob in his arms as he said, "I received an award from the gas company the other day for the greatest increase in sales in the state for our company. A Mr. Fred Little gave us the award and stated that we would be honored at some conference in a couple of months as well. That part did not bother me, but the second part is what we are debating and would appreciate your input. If you look at this plan of what they want to do to the station, you will get an idea of what they have offered and what they want. They are willing to pay for all the remodeling and adding the new wing for free. They want us to add a convenience store onto the bays and be open from five in the morning until eleven at night."

Jake exclaimed, "Wow! That must have been a surprise to have them offer that for you.

Homer seemed a little hesitant as he put together his thoughts, "It was something that they had never given me a clue about until he stopped by. They want me to go and see a similar store in action, so I can understand what it will take to run it and give it an inventory. I would own the store inventory that was not an oil product and he told me that there is a good profit in that part. There would be a coffee island and baked goods for people on their way to work. The whole thing sounds wonderful, but I would need several other people to handle that many hours per week."

Alice added, "It would change the entire character of the service station and the people we would be serving. They want to give us new pumps, so we can put gas in four vehicles at once. I do not think that Homer wants to stop repairing cars for his customers yet and tire sales are nearly half the income from that side of the business. I know that we would be handling a great deal more money, but would we be making any more in the end."

"I think that maybe the two of you should go and see what it would be like to run such a store before you decide one way or the other," Jake said. "I believe that it is a great opportunity for the two of you, but you would become a businessman more than a mechanic and there is nothing wrong with that."

Homer listened to his uncle and was going to call Mr. Little to see an operating store right away. Homer looked down at Rob in his arms and asked him if he was okay with the decision and he just pursed his lips while sleeping. Homer asked his uncle and aunt to wait a minute because he wanted to show them something. He had Flora take the baby, so he could have Alice also. He went to the back pantry and came back in with the gift box and said, "I am worse than a kid and I can't wait to give this to Alice for her birthday. This is a little early, but it may be a bigger surprise that way."

Alice just smiled and took the box from him. She gingerly removed the ribbon and lifted the cover to the box. She gasped as she could see in it. She said, "Homer, this is beautiful." She put the box on the table and lifted the necklace from it and held it up for them to see. She placed it around her neck and then lifted the earrings out and put them on. It was beautifully set off by her blue eyes in even this dim light of the evening. She walked over and gave Homer a big kiss and hug.

Homer said, "I wanted to give you a gift that you did not need for a change. Something given to you from me that you did not need and let you know how much I love you."

Jake and Flora commented on how lovely it looked as they gave Rob back to Alice and went home for the night.

Homer called Fred Little in the morning and arranged to go

fifty miles to the next state and see a store like what they wanted him to do. Homer told him that they were both going to go and planned on coming home for the night. A date was set, and he asked his uncle to check on the guys in the middle of the day while he was gone. They put an extra blanket in the back seat for Alice to get under as she would feed Rob along the way. They arrived in the early morning and were met by Mr. Little. He introduced him to the owner and gave them a short tour of what had been done to get this store open. The one thing that caught Homer's eye immediately was the fact that the cooler was massive with reach-in glass doors. The extra stock was already cold behind the shelves that people would get their stuff from. The store had a rear door with access to the cooler immediately inside for deliveries. Homer asked Mr. Little if the design could be refigured with the cooler on the end toward the neighbors, so the deliveries did not have to come through the door as this one was. He was told that they could have a serious look at why or why that would not work in his case. Mr. Little said that he had to leave now but he would call Homer in the morning at the garage to see if he had any other questions. They then got to speak to the owner about the amount of help he needed to maintain the hours of business and what he felt was the best part of the transition.

The owner said, "I was fortunate in finding someone with some history in stocking a store and keeping it manned. You might as well call him my manager because I do not change any decisions that he makes in operations here. I find that the coffee and bakery bar has been my best draw for customers. I have a group of regulars that come here for coffee and bakery items every day they go to work. I have a cashier in the morning and a person to man the coffee bar and makes sandwiches by ten in the morning. If they have extra time, they put new stock up into the shelving from the rear and do not stop the flow of the customers moving in the store. I have the flow of traffic down to the point where I know when I need two people in the yard to pump gas and they know that they are going to clean the store or remove garbage during the slow times. I have a total of four people for the first eight hours and then I let one go for the rest of the day. My manager works an average of eight hours Monday through Friday and comes in four hours on Saturday. He keeps the money on deposit, pays the dealers, and handles any schedule changes sickness may cause. Finding and keeping help can be a problem at first but I now have a good team that I pay well and that makes them loyal."

Homer said, "I have already figured out that paying my people a fair wage is worth doing. I don't see any service bays here."

The owner stated, "I created this place without wanting to offer mechanical services. It was never in my plans, and it has worked for me."

Homer and Alice asked a few more questions about how to find products for the store as they watched how the day progressed at the store. The owner said, "Do not be afraid to play hard with the retailers that will come knocking on your door. You usually can get the best prices if you do not use just one distributor for your entire product. You can get them competing for your shelf space and it pays you more money to do that. The last thing that I would tell you is to take advantage of keeping your invoices paid on time but use all the time they allow to keep your cash flow at its best. The distributors that I pay at the time of delivery give me an extra discount for doing that. I hope that I have been of some assistance today, but I must go to another appointment now."

Homer thanked him saying, "Thank you for all your help and we have to go home tonight so we are probably going to go right now as well."

Homer and Alice drove home from the store, and they certainly had a lot to talk about but they both wanted to make the changes.

Chapter Twenty-Two

Mr. Little came by the station in two days with a revision of the plan for the addition and change to a convenience store. He had placed the entire cooler toward the neighbor's lot and added a door to that side. He had placed the men's and women's bathrooms toward the street and the hall to them ended at the new door. You would enter the cooler from the hallway, so no deliveries would upset the flow of traffic. The office became next to the service bays and had a utility room behind it and the exterior wall. The coffee island moved a little closer to the cashier and there was room for several racks as well. The entire conversion of the plan met with Homer's agreement. The only thing left was to plan the timing of the remodeling.

Homer asked Ron to come into the office shortly after Mr. Little had left. Homer said, "Ron, you have been a very loyal employee over the years. I have a major change about to happen at the service station and I need to hear from you first. We are about to tear off the office and expand the building to create a convenience store to go along with the service station. I know that you probably do not want anything to do with that, but you have spoken of getting done working in the past and stayed on to teach these two kids with me. You have taught them a great deal and I would like you to continue working as long as you want to, but I am asking you first about your plans."

Ron's answer was, "I have seen a lot of changes over the years, and they have been good. I would like to keep working but maybe go down to three days per week for a little while. I do know of a good mechanic that you could hire if you liked him. How soon are you going to start building?

Homer said, "I just approved the design for them to apply to the town for the remodeling. Then we will schedule the work as soon as possible and it will be a mess for a while. They bring in a control trailer to use for an office as the work is going on. I will have to arrange to have the money removed before we lock up at night. I hope to keep the service station going as well because of our loyal customers. I will have to train one of the boys to do estimates and scheduling for the times that I will not be here. Do you think that one of the boys would do a better job than the other?"

Ron quickly stated, "Frank has been here longer, and he has a good head on his shoulders. You will have to decide, and I will have to get back to you about when I want to cut down my schedule."

Ron went back to work, and he sent the two guys out to see Homer. Glen asked if Homer had sent for them, and they were invited to have a seat for a couple of minutes.

Homer said, "I want to speak to the two of you and it may be difficult if we have a lot of gas customers in the next little while. I want to start by telling the two of you how much I appreciate the work you do for me. I have made a major decision about the service station and things are about to change."

Homer showed them the design of the new store and what was going to happen. He discussed the fact that he wanted to keep the service station open during and after the changes. Then he got down to the fact that he was going to have to train one of them to do estimates and scheduling of work. He told them that he was probably going to hire some people to just do the gas pumping and operations of the store, but they would still have to watch that the pumps were kept manned. He asked them if either one of them wanted to learn how to do estimates or scheduling. Frank said he was interested, but Glen said he did not feel qualified to tell people what to do because of persistent shyness. It was decided that the training would begin immediately and that there might be a new mechanic coming on as well.

Homer, Alice, and Rob were in church on Sunday morning listening to the preaching by Pastor Mike. Alice was proudly wearing the necklace and earrings that she had gotten for her birthday. They had gotten in the habit of fellowshipping with other couples after the service. Today would be no exception and Homer started to tell some of their friends about the changes that were about to happen at the service station. He was talking about some of the people that he would have to hire to man the store including someone with store experience if possible. He also mentioned needing to find someone to do the coffee and bakery island early in the day. He told their friends that if they knew of someone who wanted or needed work to get in touch with them. He had not left the fellowship hall when Ken Manning came over to speak to him.

Ken said, "I would like to speak to you about operating your store for you. I have done similar work while I was growing up for my parents and I would be interested in knowing what you need in an employee."

They set a time to meet during the week and then they both went home. Homer went home and made a list of his rabbits and pens and decided that he would put them up for sale now. He was beginning to think that he was going to not have time for too many side jobs soon.

Homer went into the house and found Alice resting in her chair and Rob in his crib. He took off his shoes, so he would be quieter as he went to his table used as a desk and started to look at some paperwork. He was thinking that it was time to hire a company to help with the books and especially payroll. He could take care of paying a few invoices per week, but it was going to get worse. It also crossed his mind that he had not gotten permission from the bank to do this yet, but he knew they would be in favor. The original note was more than half paid off because of the performance of the service station and it would only get better now. Alice spoke to him and asked him if he was ready to eat. Homer told her he was and then they discussed whether to hire her father for their needs and Alice still did not want to. She told Homer that what they would need was a CPA who could keep all the taxes in order as well as doing the daily stuff. She told him that she would get the name of a trusted one for him the next day.

Homer called ahead of making his deposit on Monday to speak to the loan officer he knew. They did not have any problems with the addition and encouraged him to go ahead with it. The man also told Homer that if he needed a loan for some of the inventory that he could apply for enough to keep his cash flow safe. Homer thanked him and said he would get back to him later. Homer did ask him if he knew of a good CPA in the area that he could hire. He was given the name of Bess Bartles as a person he could trust completely.

Things were moving at an incredible pace and Homer was sitting at home on a Sunday afternoon and speaking to Alice. They had just come and gotten the rabbit pens and all the rabbits from the shed after Homer sold them. "I am glad that they are gone," Homer said, "because I don't like it if I don't have the time to care for my animals the way they should be cared for. We are spending so much time interviewing people for work to help Ken Manning with the store and Frank with the gas pumps that we have not had much time to see each other. How are you doing with the new system that Bess Bartles wants us to use so we match her system?"

Alice replied, "It really is simple once you get used to it. I will be able to teach you how to enter things like the checks and the deposits very quickly. Did you see Rob trying to roll over in his crib there?"

Homer glanced at his son as he said, "I can't believe that they tore the old part down and had the shell and roof up in less than a week. I got another imprinter from the bank, and we made a mount for it at the island to save the guys some steps during the rush times. The gas rep we have now was barely able to get any pictures of what we had before they started the work. I like the new mechanic Larry and he works well with the others. I have been helping Frank get used to telling the guys what work is due to come in next and he is doing most of the invoices for the shop. Ken and I are meeting with several distributors this week and getting ready to place our first orders. The one distributor that both Ken and I want to be exclusive with is our coffee dealer who is willing to put in the automatic coffee makers if we use their product exclusively. The rest of them will have to bid on our shelf space if they want us to sell any of their products. One of the ladies at the church wants us to use some of her baked goods on the island and I may give them a try if we can keep them fresh. I don't get to take an afternoon nap like you do these days."

Alice pouted as she said, "All you must do is take care of the baby and I will go in and do some of what you are doing. I will be glad when they start making a computer that people can buy and not just businesses. Do you hear us griping over what it takes to be blessed by Jesus? We should be ashamed of ourselves when we catch ourselves doing it and repent as soon as we can."

Frank and Glen were just finishing another certification for the work they did on car electronics. Larry already had the certification from the last place that he worked at. The one thing that Larry brought to the shop that no one liked was some of the language that he would turn loose with if he were angry. Frank had taken him aside with Homer one day and they put down the rules against the language. Homer told him that there had never been any of that language there since his grandfather had started the service station and he was not in favor of having his customers hear it either. Larry told them that he would try to watch his words in the future. Frank was also training two more part-time gas pump attendees and was splitting some of the weekends with Glen so they each had one for a while and then they would switch so they both knew what was required of them.

Homer, Alice, Rob, Jake, and Flora had been to the Sunday service with Pastor Mike and were meeting at the service station as it neared being finished. Most of the equipment was in and the coolers were already being tested for their ability to stay cold. The coffee island was polished with two coffee makers waiting to make their customers happy. A new cash register was sitting by the door waiting to start collecting money. Jake said, "This is definitely a big step into the future from what Dad started."

Homer said, "I wouldn't be doing this if you hadn't believed in me Uncle Jake. I was content snaring rabbits to eat and fishing occasionally but that seems like a lifetime ago. I have gone from a lonely young man to a happily married father and businessman. I know I wanted life to be different, but I never planned on being at this point in just a couple of years. I feel like I should have paid you more for what I have now."

Jake smiled as he said, "I may have helped you get started and my belief in you was something that everyone needs in their life. Flora and I have everything that we need to live with, and we are still paying the taxes on the farm, so we still have a home to live in. The biggest difference in your life came from your momma. She made you hungry for more before you knew what it was. It is that hunger to change your life that has gotten some of this for you and the other is the blessing of our Lord, Jesus Christ. The way to make anything grow including ideas is to feed its hunger like you did in learning how to read."

Homer contemplated, "I wonder what momma would say if she could see me now with all the changes. I wonder what she would say to know that Jed and I have met and gotten to know each other some. The anger took all that Jesus had meant for her to enjoy while on earth. I cannot be mad at her because she made me who I am, and I loved her until she died because she was my momma. Did you see the safe in the office over there?"

The oil company said they would help to pay for a big open house for the opening of the new store with Homer. It had been open for ten days so far and most of the bugs of the new machinery and staffing questions had been worked on already when it was to be held. The one thing that several people had suggested did not please Homer, but his CPA had confirmed was the store receiving a new name. It was taken from Baker's Service Station to now being Baker's Quick Stop and Service Station on legal documents and Baker's Quick Stop on their signage. They decided that they would make a day of the festivities on Saturday with free food and things for children to do outside of the store. They got several of their vendors to chip in on some of the costs of the food they were going to serve.

Homer, Alice, Rob, Jake, and Flora were there with the oil company rep to cut ceremonial red tape for photographers at ten o'clock in the morning. It was a very confusing but fun time for most of the people involved. Ken was given the job of overseeing the free food as well as having things in order in the store. Frank was there for the ceremony and was interviewed about what services were available for vehicles from his team of workers by the photographers.

Homer was greeting some of the customers as they milled around the store and was surprised to find a couple of faces that he remembered. Jimmy Taylor came by and made a point of speaking to Homer, but he was much less derogatory in his tone for this conversation. He congratulated Homer on what he had done with his life after the childhood that he had had. They shook hands as Jimmy left the store. The other person that Homer was surprised to see was Rachael from the days of swimming in her pond and he had to notice that she had finished growing up since he last had seen her. He introduced her to Alice and Rob before she left the store. Homer looked around at some of the other people who had gathered there, and he saw Jake speaking to his father-in-law in the front yard. The judge waved hello to him as their eyes met for a few seconds. Alice was speaking to her parents as they played with Rob in the yard. It seemed to be a phenomenally successful day at having achieved its purpose. They even got a blessing over the store from Pastor Mike as he and Mary stopped in to say hello. Homer was glad to think that he could get some extra rest after the service tomorrow.

Homer and Alice quickly realized that keeping the paperwork straight with this amount of volume was going to be a little more difficult. It took an average of two hours or more just to list the credit cards for deposit in the right places. They met with the gas company rep and found that they could give the gas delivery driver sealed bags of credit card receipts at any time and settle with the rep every two weeks instead of weekly. That eliminated one deadline from the bookkeeping. The cash register made it, so they could calculate what was being sold on any given day and see if there were any mistakes being made before it all got out of hand. It was going to take a while to figure out if they were making enough money to offset the time required to control this beast and its man hours. Homer and Alice had one of their worst arguments about how to get the paperwork done and who was going to be responsible. They ended up giving Ken the job of doing some of the balancing of accounts from the register tapes.

Homer, Alice, Jake, and Flora all got together one evening to see how they could get some time for themselves in all this mess. Jake pointed out that it would probably be a while before they could hire a bookkeeper to ease their burden but that was what it was going to take. Homer turned the question around and said, "What hours are being done by whom would we have to change to be able to afford a bookkeeper? Could we adjust what Ken is doing with some of his time and maybe even Frank?"

Jake said, "You may have a good point there. If all the information of any given day were placed in the hands of a bookkeeper instead of your managers, it would free them up to do other things and help maintain the bottom line as a profit. You need to create a way to post the credit cards to the deposit slips more efficiently than you are doing now. They need to come up with a machine that tells the bank about the transaction accurately without having to handle the information as much using one person. I'll bet that someone is already working on that problem."

Homer decided that if he was going to have any quality time with his wife and son, he was going to have to follow up on his options. He decided that he would ask Mr. Moodie for his advice about the situation and see what he could come up with for him. He would get with Ken and Frank as soon as he could. He decided that he would also ask at the bank if there was a way to make this easier for everyone. He did not like the strain that the new work was putting on them and he wanted that to change. Homer knew that ultimately it was up to him to create some of the change in his life and he was serious about this.

Ken was the one that Homer found could change the most hours in the whole scheme of manning the store. To have a bookkeeper balance the days accounting would free him up a great deal to handle inventory easier and eliminate at least three-man hours per day from peripheral staff. Frank would be able to do more mechanical work but could not change his staff. The rest of the time would have to be creatively found to help pay for a bookkeeper. A week later, Homer gave up most of his office to a part time worker. He decided to share part of the office in the service bays for his work.

Chapter Twenty-Three

Homer was sitting with a customer representative at his bank after making a deposit. They were discussing the magnitude of labor involved with the taking of credit cards without considering the fees being charged for each transaction. The bank rep was empathizing with Homer and asked him a question. Homer was asked if he wanted to be one of the clients that the bank would test a new system with. Homer asked her to explain the details to him to think about. She asked him if he had noticed cards coming through in the last few years with a black stripe on the back and Homer said yes. She told him that there was a machine that now could read a message from that strip and convey a great deal of information from it. She said that she would not bore him with all it could read but it used a telephone connection to the bank. It would tell the bank who the person was to be charged, Homer would punch in the amount on a keypad, and it would get recorded to his accounts. She handed Homer a sheet of paper spelling out how it worked as she continued to speak. She told Homer that it was still going to have fees involved with the transaction, but he would not have to enter each one of the cards separately. Homer asked her about the credit cards issued by his gas company and how they would have to be handled. The rep told him that they could program the machine to accept cards for one other company card if he wanted to for the same fees. The difference would be that the funds would be sent directly to the gas company and not his accounts. By now Homer was smiling and asked if she was telling him a story? The rep assured him that it was real, and he could be one of the first in the area to help them try it all out. Homer asked her for a sheet comparing the fees for him and Alice to consider but he was extremely interested in doing it.

Homer and Alice did not need awfully long to consider the use of the new machine to take credit cards. Homer called his gas suppliers and got them involved in direct contact with the bank, so they would have the correct information to use. The biggest hassle was getting a second telephone line into the store, so it could be used by the machine at once. Ken and the new bookkeeper, Naomi Perkins, were getting trained in how to work the machine and how the paperwork would differ. It then had to be aligned with what Bess Bartles wanted as a format. Homer was sure that once it was all working that it would be much easier and quicker to find a mistake and get it finished correctly. Even when he hired Naomi, it seemed to be a perfect fit for their needs. Naomi was a single mom and had to have some flexibility in her schedule to manage to keep working if one of her children had a need while she was at work. Homer respected the fact that she had not allowed her children to be separated after her husband walked out on her. He knew that his childhood could have been different if his momma had done similarly so he was glad to hire Naomi. Ken would be responsible for training his cashiers on the machine.

Homer spent a great deal of time encouraging the people

that worked for him. He would take time to listen to some of the reasons that they were working and tried to help those that needed it the most. There was also one side of this job that became bothersome to him. He knew that some of the people he had hired were willing to steal from him. Some of the new ones thought that anything in the store was for their consumption while they were there working without paying for it. Homer would have Ken speak to them about paying for what they wanted and if they insisted on continuing the activity, they were fired immediately. It has become necessary to implement a trial period of employment for each new employee.

The first couple of months after the new machine did get installed were a nightmare for his managers and for Homer. There was a lag time from imprinting the cards in the machine and their knowing where the money went for certain. Naomi tried her best to get the information from the cash register, but it took a lot of her time. Homer went to the bank on more than one occasion to try and get the system working better for everyone involved. It clearly took less time to get the deposits done but the separating of accounts was difficult until the bank got the program to print out the daily numbers and where they went. This brought the lag time done to two days and proved to be manageable.

While the store was being established, the service station was going strong. Frank was getting new clients on a regular basis because of the exposure to more people. Homer negotiated with a tire wholesaler in the next town for better pricing on tires if he would install some of the tires that the wholesalers needed installed for an agreed price. This diminished their stocking requirements to ease the lack of storage in the service station now. Once the clients got their tires done there, it was easier to have them get their other work done there as well.

Homer was working in his back office when a slightly elder lady came in to speak to him. She was pleasantly dressed, and her hair was done nicely in a bun. She said, "Are you the owner, sir?"

Homer looked at her and said, "Yes ma'am I am. What can I do for you this lovely day?"

She said, "My name is Edith Godin, and I would like to come to work for you if I could. I have worked all my life, but I can no longer be employed where I was because of my age. I love being around the public and I would like to know if I could work at your coffee bar in the morning. I do not mean to be cruel but the young lady you have working there now has the personality of a doorknob. You can use it, but it has no desires. She should be speaking to the regulars and making them welcome as they use your store daily. I would like you to give me a try in that position and you will not be sorry."

Homer had sat quietly listening to the woman. He smiled as he asked, "The personality of a doorknob is what you think? I am still new at being a store owner but what you have said makes sense. Do you think that you could keep up the pace and for how long daily?"

Edith said, "I would like to work all six days of the week for four to six hours and I can run circles around your youngsters in there now. I lost my husband a couple of years ago, so I have no other obligations during the day. It would give meaning back to my life and I would serve you well."

Homer decided to have Ken come back and meet her because he was still letting Ken do the hiring of the store help. When Ken heard her story, he was more than glad to let her come on board and he would give the other young lady a try at some other work and teach her how to be around customers.

Homer made it a point to go in and watch his people for a couple of days without being too obvious. He was pleasantly surprised to hear some of the banter that the customers would do with Edith. Many of the young men liked to be called by name and smiled at by a motherly matron. He also noticed the difference in some of his cashiers at the front door. Everyone saw this person and if they were spoken to, they were more likely to get more items and come back again. He would have to speak to Ken about one of their people and see if she could change her speech and facial expressions.

The time came for the oil companies' convention. Homer, Alice, and Rob were going to be presented with the plaque that was already hanging in the office in a formal dinner. They had asked Homer to give a short speech to other gas station owners with some encouragement for them. The oil company had some slides they were going to show of the original station, the revised old station, and the new store in operation while Homer did his speech.

Mr. Fred Little brought everyone up to date on the evening program and then started. He said, "We have some special people that we want you all to meet tonight. His grandfather started the service station nearly thirty-five years ago while this young man was only a hope in his father's eye. He did not grow up anywhere near the station because his father went to work for the mines until his early death. His Uncle Jake took over the service station when his father died and ran it for many years. I do not want to spoil what our special guest has to say so I will just introduce you to Homer, Alice, and Rob Baker."

On their cue, the three of them went up onto the stage amidst a great hand clapping and whistles. They then turned and looked out at the mass of people who were in attendance and Homer started to get nervous.

Mr. Little said, "We are going to ask Alice and Rob to stay here for a minute because we have two presentations to do before we hear from Homer. Homer, I would like to present to you this plaque for the most increased gas sales for any station in one year." Another round of thunderous clapping from the audience and then Mr. Little raised his hand for silence. "We also have found out that you believed in us as an oil company from the very beginning. You invested in stocks with our company years ago and have been a faithful partner with our growth. To honor your support in a more tangible way, we are going to double the number of shares that you own as a gift from us."

Another round of clapping as Homer took the certificate and handed it to Alice to take back to their seats. Homer just stood there a second before he said, "I have been asked to encourage some of you tonight, so I thought that I might tell you a little about myself. My father did work for the mines near where I live now. I do not remember him because of how young I was when he died. My mother became very depressed after his death and did some things I have since found out about. I recently found out that she gave away a younger brother to another family to cherish as their own. His name was Jed and named after my grandfather. When his adoptive father died, he came looking for the mother who had given him away at birth. He did not find her because my momma died of a stroke a few months before he came walking into our house. My momma died a horrible death and lived a worse life. She became angry at God for having taken her husband and she died angry nearly twenty years later. My momma and I lived in a tar paper shack on my uncle's farm because she would not live in a house given to her for charity. I never went to school and at the age of twenty could not read or write. This is the time when I received the most encouraging words of my life from my Uncle Jake, and he helped me turn my life around. His words to me were that I was not stupid as my momma assumed but was merely unlearned. He gave me a job in the service station and hired a private teacher to secretly teach me how to read and write. By then, I was hungry for a new life, and I studied every chance that I could. We had always eaten off the land and I also learned that there were other things to eat and drink. I was twenty-one years old when I had my first cranberry sauce with a turkey dinner. I loved what I was learning, and I wanted to learn more. This is the time when my uncle decided that I had learned enough to take over the service station from him. You can see on the wall what it looked like at that time. I bought the station and had the new pumps and facelift done while I was away on my honeymoon. I must take a minute here to tell you what God can do if you have a pure heart and a pure love for your wife. There is no stronger partnership than one founded on love. With the new pumps and the facelift, we did earn the distinction of increasing our sales more than anyone else in the state for that year. You can see what it looked like when they got done with the first changes. But for some reason, they believed that I could do more, and they sent Mr. Little to make me an offer again. Please show the last slide now. This is my service station now with a convenience store attached to it. We need to have gas delivered an average of three times per week now. We employ more than twenty people if you count our part-time personnel. All this came about from someone saying, Homer, you are not stupid but unlearned. You combine that with a faithful, inspiring wife and a personal determination to want things to be different and this is what can happen. Thank you very much."

Homer, Alice, Rob, Jake, Flora, and Jed were all sitting around the Thanksgiving table after eating their fill. Rob was pounding on the tray of his highchair with the handle of his spoon and using the other hand to feed himself with his fingers. Homer said, "I took a nice quiet walk this morning to thank God for all he has done for us this year. I thanked him that all of you are an influence in my life for its fulfillment. I even thanked God for my momma and her influence in my life and for her giving Jed a life away from us. I do not believe that there is a self-made man as the world believes. We all learn to act or react to our history. I am only glad that the future can be changed and not dependent on our history."

Everyone at the table let out a cry of agreement and all said, "TO OUR FUTURE!!!"

Made in the USA
Columbia, SC
06 March 2024

32827676R20148